"Let's Get This Settled Tonight.

Tom's house is at the end of this road. Let's stop in."

Ryder laughed. "Look at yourself. Your attorney will probably think you've just been mugged. Even worse, he might think you and I have—"

"Tom wouldn't think anything of the kind! Besides, seeing him is more important to me than worrying if every hair is in place."

"You've got much more than just a hair out of place, honey," Ryder declared. "Good ol' Tom might really wonder what went on out there on the road. His homecoming queen looks like she's just had a nice roll in the mud. Your hair's a mess, your blouse is all wet and it's halfway undone. . . ."

JANET JOYCE

resides in Ohio and is happily married to the man who swept her off her feet as a college coed; she admits that her own romance is what prompted her writing career. She and her family like camping and traveling, and are avid fans of college football. Ms. Joyce is an accomplished pianist, enjoys composing her own lyrics and reads voraciously.

Dear Reader:

SILHOUETTE DESIRE is an exciting new line of contemporary romances from Silhouette Books. During the past year, many Silhouette readers have written in telling us what other types of stories they'd like to read from Silhouette, and we've kept these comments and suggestions in mind in developing SILHOUETTE DESIRE.

DESIREs feature all of the elements you like to see in a romance, plus a more sensual, provocative story. So if you want to experience all the excitement, passion and joy of falling in love, then SILHOUETTE DESIRE is for you.

Karen Solem
Editor-in-Chief
Silhouette Books

JANET JOYCE
Controlling Interest

Silhouette Desire
Published by Silhouette Books New York
America's Publisher of Contemporary Romance

Silhouette Books by Janet Joyce

Winter Lady (DES #53)
Man of the House (DES #71)
Man of Glory (DES #98)
Controlling Interest (DES #116)

SILHOUETTE BOOKS, a Division of Simon & Schuster, Inc.
1230 Avenue of the Americas, New York, N.Y. 10020

ISBN: 0-671-47382-4

First Silhouette Books printing February, 1984

10 9 8 7 6 5 4 3 2 1

America's Publisher of Contemporary Romance

Printed in the U.S.A.

Controlling
Interest

1

Cattails waved on either side of the narrow two-lane road that cut across the marshy backwater along the shores of Lake Erie. A startled white heron took flight when an aging red convertible shot down the lonely stretch of road and swerved to avoid a pothole in the pavement. Laura Davis pressed her foot down on the Mustang's accelerator, anxious to complete the final leg of her trip from Chicago to the small resort town of Mainport, Ohio.

A stray tendril of blond hair dipped over her forehead, and she brushed it away, blinking back the tears that threatened behind her amber-flecked gray eyes. How many times in the past had she taken this short cut down the old harbor road? So many times she couldn't count, but this time was different, for Grandpa Davis wouldn't be waiting to welcome her home to the Cliffs.

The cool breeze ruffling her long hair would normally

have had an exhilarating effect on her. But tonight she was oblivious to the stark, wild beauty of the marshland, distracted by memories from the past, memories of her grandfather and the rambling Victorian house he had converted into a small inn. Frowning, she contemplated the next day's meeting with Tom Anderson, her grandfather's attorney, wondering why the letter she'd received from him implied such urgency. Her grandfather's will had already been read, and she was the sole heir, so why did Tom think there were problems? She shrugged off the nagging thoughts that had troubled her for days and let her mind wander back to happier times, days of swimming in the lake, fishing off the pier, dancing beneath a yellow August moon.

Laura had grown up at the Cliffs. After her parents' deaths in a tragic boating accident during a summer storm on the lake, she'd been raised by her grandparents. Her grandmother had died while Laura was in college, and she had immediately offered to return home to help out at the inn, but Gramps had insisted she complete her studies and receive her degree in education.

After graduation, she had again offered to come back, but her grandfather had argued against it, saying she should take the teaching job she'd been offered in Chicago, since he was very capable of managing the inn alone. She'd wanted to visit in the summers, but he'd obstinately decreed that a young woman like Laura shouldn't waste her time at a quiet family resort like the Cliffs but enjoy the social life to be found in the city. Laura had finally accepted that decision and spent only the two weeks she had between the regular term and the summer remedial sessions she taught vacationing at the inn.

Her grandfather's sudden death had occurred just as Laura was beginning to realize that she couldn't face another term at the inner-city school where she'd been assigned for four years. Despite the absence of her grandfather, she was looking forward to the peaceful serenity to be found at the Cliffs, hoping her battered emotions would soon be well on the road to recovery. A deep love for children had initially drawn her to elementary education, but that same love had forced her to give up teaching. She'd made the tragic mistake of giving too much of herself to her students, and their needs were not only educational and practical but emotional. They desperately needed the sincere affection of a concerned adult, but she realized now that she couldn't return to teaching until she'd regained some of her objectivity.

After her grandfather's funeral, Laura had made the decision to give up her job before the start of the new term. She'd flown back to Chicago, resigned, packed all of her belongings, and a week later was ready to return to her childhood home.

The only thing that was causing her any anxiety was that letter from Tom. The letter stated that there had been new developments since the reading of her grandfather's will. According to the letter, management of the inn had been placed in the hands of one Wilson R. Bantel not long before Merrill Davis's death, but she'd never heard the man's name mentioned before and had no idea why her grandfather would have put a stranger in charge of the family-held business. Supposedly, Bantel represented a consulting firm in hotel management that had been contracted by her grandfather, but Laura didn't think the Cliffs needed an expensive consultant. The letter had gone on to say that Bantel had offered to buy the Cliffs, but she had no intention of selling. She planned to dismiss the man and his firm as soon as she could. She regretted that she'd been too grief-stricken during the week of the funeral to question who was managing the inn but felt confident she could clear up any misunderstanding as soon as she returned home.

Her contemplation came to an abrupt end when a slow-moving pickup truck came into view ahead of her. After following it impatiently for a few minutes, Laura decided to pass. She swerved across the center line, but another car was coming from the opposite direction, and she was forced to brake and stay behind the dusty blue truck.

A short time later, she had another opportunity to pass, but when she was about to swing into the other lane, the plodding truck weaved across the middle of the road, blocking her way.

"Give me a break," Laura snapped, jamming her palm down on the horn, but the driver didn't seem to notice. It seemed an inordinately long time before the lumbering vehicle allowed her to pass.

Her irritation superseded her judgment, and she pressed the gas pedal to the floor. As she came alongside the driver's window, she glared at the dark-haired man scowling down at her, then pointedly left him behind in a cloud of dust. Swerving into the lane ahead, she didn't reduce speed until she could no longer see the truck in her rear-view mirror.

Passing the first of an increasing number of billboards and signs along the road, Laura relaxed. She was nearing town, and it wouldn't be long before her hot, tiring trip would be over. She couldn't wait to strip off her sticky clothes and immerse herself in a soothing tub of warm water. With that comforting thought in mind, she speeded up until a sudden vibration in the steering wheel told her there might be a delay in her plans.

"Don't fail me now, baby," she crooned pleadingly, but the car began slowing and was soon sputtering like a choke victim. Having no other choice, she steered to the side of the road and rolled to a stop on the narrow shoulder.

"Damn!" she groaned, realizing she was still well over two miles away from town and had no idea what was wrong with her car. She'd checked the fuel gauge when she'd passed through the last town and had filled up her tank, so that couldn't possibly be the problem. When she glanced at the gauge, however, it read empty.

Stepping out of the car, she looked back down the road and discovered her problem. A wet trail of fuel slowly trickled from beneath her car. Walking around the fender, she bent down and ascertained that she'd broken a fuel line somewhere along the rough road. In the gathering dusk, she accepted the discouraging fact that there was nothing to do but stay in her car and wait for some passer-by to come to her aid.

The minutes seemed to drag into hours as she listened to the din of croaking frogs in the swampy marsh off the road. A swarm of gnats descended over her head, and she was too busy swatting bugs to notice that the wheels of her car were rapidly sinking in the mud. Heeding the warning drone of oncoming mosquitoes, she got out of the car and began struggling to put up the top. Her heels sinking in the soft ground, she clumsily began fastening the heavy-duty snaps, but before she was able to complete the job, she'd broken a fingernail and been bitten several times by the greedy insects.

Scratching one of the reddened swellings on her arm, she climbed back into the car and quickly rolled up the windows, but it was a warm and muggy August evening, and beads of perspiration were soon rolling down her flushed face.

"That does it," she decreed when a thin trickle of moisture rolled down between her breasts. Deciding it would be better to walk into town than suffocate in her car, she pulled open the glove compartment and found a flashlight. She picked up her purse, then stepped out into what was fast becoming an inky, starless night.

Hurriedly, she locked up her car and began walking, fighting back tears of frustration when the mosquitoes honed in on her flight and renewed their attack full force.

"Damn, damn, damn," she wailed, and quickened her pace, swatting wildly at the black battalion of bloodthirsty insects intent on devouring her. Hardly able to see where she was going, she misjudged her footing, lost her balance, and lurched forward. Her tender palms were cut by the gravel as she instinctively tried to break her fall, ending up on all fours on the mucky ground. Feeling the sting in her scraped hands and knees, the wet soil soaking into the material of her green linen skirt, she forced herself back on her heels. Biting her lip, she brushed off her hands and felt trickles of blood running down her legs.

"What else can happen?" She groped for her purse and the flashlight, finding them close by. Unfortunately, the small handkerchief she carried did little to wipe the grit from her injured hands and knees.

Two beams of light from an oncoming vehicle gave her the chance to estimate the damage she'd done to herself, but she didn't stop to make more repairs, scrambling to her feet. Waving her flashlight, she shouted for the driver to stop, praying the car would see her and not run her down. With growing dismay, she recognized the familiar outline of a rattletrap truck.

"Wouldn't you know it?" she questioned the small sliver of moon, shaking her head as the noisy vehicle slowed down and stopped behind her car. It would have to be him, she thought disgustedly, and slowly started limping back the way she had come.

The driver jumped down from the cab, holding a battery-operated lantern over his head. It shone like a spotlight in comparison with her dim flashlight and illuminated the scowling features of the man who carried it. His frown hadn't smoothed since the first time she had seen it, and with a sinking heart, she went to meet him. The man was tall and dark-haired, wearing a light blue work shirt rolled up to the elbows and completely unbuttoned down the front. The glow from the lantern gave her a glimpse of a wide muscular chest shadowed by curling dark hair that narrowed to a thin line down his flat stomach and disappeared into worn jeans that hugged his slim hips.

"Having trouble?" His deep voice cut through the space that separated them, and Laura tried to quell a slight shiver of apprehension. She was alone, on a little-traveled section of road, facing an intimidating stranger who might offer more than a ride into town.

"I . . . I think I've broken my fuel line," she stammered in an unnaturally high-pitched voice. "Could you stop at the next service station and send back a tow truck?"

She couldn't seem to keep her eyes off the expanse of bare skin revealed by his loose shirt fluttering free in the slight breeze off the backwater. Although she feared her expression revealed the panicky trend of her thoughts, his face revealed nothing as he calmly bent down and shone the lantern under her car.

"I think you're probably right," His tone was grudging. "But by the time I'd get back here with a tow truck, the mosquitoes will've carried you off bit by bit."

He stood up and brushed the back of his hand over his brow. "Let's get in my truck and find a station that'll send somebody back for your car." He swatted at his neck, the mosquitoes turning their attack on him. "Come on. If this heat doesn't get us, the bugs will."

Before she could reply, he closed the space between them and lifted the lantern, shining the light into her eyes. She suddenly felt like a very rumpled Red Riding Hood confronted with a dangerous wolf as his eyes raked over her, appraising every inch of her figure.

"I don't want to leave my car unattended," she hedged, taking a step back. Her hand groped for the door handle, but she had forgotten that she'd locked up the car. As soon as she opened her purse to find her keys, the weak light from her flashlight faltered and died. She swallowed a constricting bubble of hysteria. "Please, just send back a truck. I'm not in any hurry, but I'm sure you'd like to get going."

Again, he lifted the lantern to include her in the circle of yellow light. "A while back, you seemed in quite a big hurry. You almost ended up in the ditch trying to pass me on that narrow curve. Now you tell me you'd rather suffocate in your car than ride with me into town. Look, lady, you don't have to worry about accepting a ride with this stranger." His chuckle was low, vibrantly male, and totally amused. "If you haven't noticed, you're a god-awful mess."

She knew she was a bedraggled shadow of her former self, but it was certainly rude of him to point it out. Her fear quickly vanished and was replaced by her temper. "Look, mister," she retorted, "if you're going to be insulting, you can go on without me. I'll wait for the next car to help me."

"And the odds are that won't be for hours," he shot back. "Do you want to spend the night fighting off the mosquitoes in this snake-ridden swamp or do the practical thing and come with me?"

"I'm beginning to think I'd be better off staying here than going anywhere with you," Laura was stung into replying. "And that damn truck of yours is so slow it could be tomorrow before we make it into town."

Even in the dark, she could sense his annoyance. The irritated edge to his voice didn't come as a surprise, but she still felt like flinching as the cutting words lashed over her head. "I'm almost out of patience, lady. I suggest you get yourself over to that truck before I forget this is my good deed for the day and leave you to the mercy of the next guy who comes along. Maybe he won't be as hot and tired as I am and he'll take more for his trouble than you're prepared to give."

Another shiver of apprehension ran down Laura's spine as she digested his words. Could she trust him? He was arrogant, ill-tempered, and was scaring her to death, but he didn't seem the type who'd force himself on a defenseless woman. She jumped in sudden fright when a shrieking nighthawk swooped low over the marsh and flew back into the sky with a field mouse enclosed in its lethal talons. Feeling much like the helpless animal being carried away, she made her decision. "All right," she murmured softly, lifting her chin to prove he hadn't totally intimidated her.

"At last." He shrugged his shoulders and began walking to the back of her car. "I wonder if the first Good Samaritan had as much trouble getting someone to accept his help."

"If he looked anything like you, he did," Laura muttered under her breath, but the man had a keen sense of hearing.

"I'm not dangerous, lady, just tired." He flashed her a less than apologetic grin. "You might want to take anything of value with you. Your car will sit here for a while, and these convertibles are easy to break into."

She nodded, digging into her purse for her keys. It seemed to take hours, but that still didn't give him the right to grab the purse out of her shaky hands and find the keys for himself. "I'm getting eaten alive," he offered as an explanation. Still glaring at him, she reached for her small overnight bag, waited as he lifted out her heavy suitcase and reclosed the trunk, then held out her hand for her keys.

"Trusting soul, aren't you?" he asked, but dropped the keys into her hand and began walking away toward his truck.

She followed his long-legged stride, noting when he paused to let her catch up with him that she barely came up to his shoulder. He was well over six feet tall, and at five seven, it was rare for her to feel so small around men, especially in the high heels she was wearing.

Effortlessly, he hoisted her suitcase into the back of his truck, then turned to face her. A gentle but firm touch on her elbow sent a shock of electricity up her arm, but she didn't show that she was very much aware of him as a man. She could feel the heat of his body

16

emanating from the virile chest so close to her and quelled the sudden rush of feminine response that erupted within her.

He seemed oblivious to her reaction to his blatant maleness as he courteously helped her up into the cab. Not realizing how he might interpret the movement, she deliberately placed her travel case down on the seat beside her as if it would provide some kind of barrier. She jumped when he forcefully slammed her door shut with a quick swing of one muscular arm. I'm acting like a frightened idiot, Laura acknowledged to herself, watching as he strode around the front end of the truck and swung himself up onto the seat beside her. Before reaching down to start the engine, he turned his head. "Want to tell me your name, or would that make things too personal?"

"Laura," she offered. Then, reading his exasperated expression, she added, "Laura Davis."

He reached down and started the ignition, seeming to pause longer than necessary before responding in kind.

"Ryder." He offered his first name in a tone that effectively implied she shouldn't expect more, and Laura was both angered and confused. Why did he make her feel like a fool for hesitating before revealing her full name when he had no intention of telling her his?

"Ryder?" she questioned pointedly, but her answer was a full-volume blast from the radio as he began fiddling with the dial.

"Damn thing gives off more interference than music, but I like some noise when I drive. Keeps me awake." He found a station but kept the volume at a level precluding further conversation.

Taking the rude hint, Laura stiffened her spine and

gazed straight ahead. If that's the way you want it, it's fine with me, she mentally fumed, making up her mind not to say one more word to him. She could sense each time he glanced over at her, studying her profile with assessing eyes, but she stubbornly refused to look at him. She strove to appear disinterested in anything but reaching their destination. As he shifted gears, the ominous sounds from the coughing engine made her wonder if his truck had any more chance of reaching the station than her crippled car. She felt every bump in the road, and with each passing mile, the truck seemed to lose more speed.

Seeing her apprehensive expression, Ryder grinned. "She does a lot of complaining, but she won't let me down."

"You're referring to this thing you call a truck?"

"Mmm," he agreed, lovingly patting a dented section of the spattered dashboard. "All she wants is the proper handling and a little love and attention." He began to whistle softly, between his teeth, throwing her a mocking glance that made her catch her breath. It was apparent that he included her in his assessment of the best way to handle the female gender, but she didn't give him the satisfaction of an affronted feminist comment. She chafed in silence, becoming increasingly annoyed with herself for not being able to ignore him altogether. Her eyes strayed across the seat to his capable hands on the steering wheel and admired the hard muscles of his long arms when he shifted gears and the flex in his broad shoulders.

Initially, she had thought he was in his twenties, but she'd revised her assessment when she got a better look at him. He was in his thirties, with the attractive lines in his face of a man who has lived life to its fullest. He had an aura of power surrounding him, out of sync with his clothing and the dilapidated truck he was driving.

Within the close confines of the cab, she was even more aware of his size. The breadth of his shoulders seemed to take up more than his share of space, and she noticed that the seat was pushed as far back as possible to make room for his long legs. The soft faded denim of his jeans was stretched like a second skin over powerful thighs and hard calves. She had to pull her eyes away from the captivating movement of his legs as he downshifted for an upcoming hill. Sightlessly, she glanced out her window at the passing marshland, not fully understanding why she suddenly wished she looked more attractive. She bit her lip and unconsciously began brushing her soiled skirt.

Ryder regarded her activity with doubtful eyes. "I think you're wasting your time."

She couldn't think of anything to say, so she merely nodded her agreement and continued staring miserably out the window.

2

⚬⚬⚬⚬⚬⚬⚬⚬⚬⚬⚬⚬

The rushes were beginning to thin as the truck crossed the small wooden bridge that led into Mainport. A blinking neon sign marked the location of an upcoming service station.

"Here we are." Ryder turned into the station and pulled up near the open garage doors. He quickly jumped out of the cab, sauntered around to the passenger side, and was there to assist Laura before she'd figured out how to work the door handle.

"You have to have a magic touch." He took her by the hand, totally ignored her attempts to pull her fingers out of his grasp, and compelled her with him toward the lighted interior of the station. "Got a first-aid kit, Jed?" he called, not lifting his gaze from the scraped palm of her hand. "This must hurt like the devil. Why didn't you tell me your hand was bleeding? Let's see the other one."

"Let go of me." Laura had no more success getting him to release her than she'd had outside. "I'm not about to bleed to death."

She was about to say more, but a man came in through the garage door and joined them. Wiping his hands on a greasy rag, he lifted a baseball cap from his graying hair and brushed the back of his hand over his forehead. "Top drawer in the desk," the man called Jed directed, casting a sympathetic eye over Laura's besmeared clothes and bloodstained legs. "Ain't been in an accident, have ya?"

"No, nothing like that," Laura began, but was cut off by Ryder.

"Her car broke down on the way in to town." Ryder again grasped her elbow and edged her toward the desk. "Sit up here. We'll get you cleaned up. Then you can tell Jed where he can find your car."

"That's hardly necessary," Laura said sharply, turning away from Ryder to the man who could help her with the car. "I'd appreciate it— Hey!" she lost her train of thought as two large hands closed around her waist. She was lifted off her feet, then swiftly seated on the wide metal desk. "Look here . . . uh . . . Ryder. I don't think—"

"Can you get me a basin of water, Jed?" Ryder cut her off, pulling open a desk drawer and removing a metal first-aid kit.

"Sure thing." Jed disappeared into an adjoining room, and Laura heard the sound of running water.

"I didn't come here for this." She was about to hop down from the desk but decided against it when she saw the intimidating look on Ryder's face. "I can clean up at home. All I want to do is make arrangements for my . . . my car." Her words sounded subdued, and she hoped he didn't realize it was because she'd suddenly gotten her first really close look at him. He was even better looking than she'd realized. In the bright light, she could see the strong line of his jaw, his sculpted lips, and the lush, curling lashes shading his intense blue eyes. She swallowed hard and tried not to stare at the two deep dimples that grooved his cheeks.

"You're going to stay put until we get you fixed up, and that's that," Ryder informed her tersely, pulling bandages and tape from the metal box.

"Yes, sir!" Laura exclaimed waspishly, deciding his boorish personality didn't complement his looks. She admitted to herself that some of her ill temper was prompted by the realization that she had never looked worse in her life. Not a vain woman, she was nevertheless annoyed that Ryder was witness to her humiliating disarray. She bowed her head so he couldn't see her smudged face, streaked with perspiration.

She was grateful when Jed came back with the basin of water and set it down on the desk beside her. Both she and Ryder reached for the cloth Jed offered at the same time.

"I'll do it," Laura proclaimed stubbornly, embarrassed enough as it was without having to cope with Ryder's tending to her injuries.

Once again, he took matters into his own, much stronger hands, jerking the cloth out of her grasp and dipping it into the basin. Her cheeks flamed pink as he went down on one knee in front of her and began wiping the dried blood from her legs.

"I'd help out, but my hands are pretty dirty," Jed declared, rubbing his palms down his oil-stained pants.

"Tell him about your car," Ryder suggested, not shifting his gaze from the shapely contours of her legs.

"I broke down on the Old Harbor Road about five miles out of town," Laura began, wishing Ryder would hurry. It was getting harder and harder to bear the feel of his warm fingers against her skin as he tended to one leg, then the other. "It's a broken fuel line, I think."

"Rotten luck," Jed said, shaking his head as if her problems were not yet over.

"Oh." Laura gasped, sucking in her breath as Ryder began dabbing at the torn skin on her knee. Instinctively, she tried to move her leg away, but regretted the action as soon as Ryder slipped his hand behind her knee and took a firm grasp. His warm fingers felt like a brand against her soft skin, and it took a great deal of will power to speak. A bit breathlessly, she again attempted to explain the situation to Jed, but he merely nodded at her, his kindly brown eyes watching Ryder as he administered to her other knee.

"Let's hold on for a few minutes," Jed finally advised. "First things first."

Sensing correctly that it would do her no good to continue, Laura suffered in silence as Ryder began treating her hands to the same gentle cleansing. "Thank you," she managed when he'd finished, thinking that at last they'd get down to business, but she quickly found out Ryder wasn't satisfied with half a job.

"This will sting," he announced, holding her gaze as he tilted some antiseptic onto a clean cotton ball.

Thinking the expression in his eyes was some kind of challenge, she tilted her chin. "I'm sure I'll live."

She could've sworn she saw his lips twitching before he knelt down and applied a liberal dose of fiery liquid to each knee. Laura had to fight back the tears as he took hold of her hand. She wouldn't let him see her cry, she just wouldn't. She told herself he'd probably laugh if she admitted how much it hurt.

"Sorry." His terse pronouncement took her by surprise, as did the tight expression on his face, as if he regretted causing her any more pain. He didn't meet her eyes, keeping his gaze centered on the torn flesh of her palm.

Looking highly uncomfortable with her plight, Jed patted her kindly on the shoulder; then, realizing his greasy fingers were leaving a mark on her white blouse, he swiftly drew back his hand. "I sure wish I could help you, ma'am, but I'm alone on duty tonight. Been an accident on the interstate, and our truck is out helpin' clear up the mess."

Laura was unable to ignore the strange tingles of pleasure-pain coursing up her arms as Ryder, having applied the antiseptic, began blowing on the stinging flesh of her palms. She listened to Jed with only half an ear, trying to concentrate but having little luck. Ryder's large hands held both of hers firmly, yet she had no desire to pull them away, her lips unconsciously parting as he lifted them into much too close a proximity with his sensuously molded lips and medicated them with his warm breath. Suddenly, he was staring directly into her eyes with his entrancing blue gaze, and a jolting current of physical awareness hit her full force.

Not wanting him to see how much she was affected by his intimate visual caress, she lowered her lashes. "How . . . how long do you think it will be, Jed?"

"I 'spect you'll have to stay on till tomorrow." Jed rubbed the back of his neck, his expression rueful. "You might have trouble gettin' a room 'cuz most places are full up this time of year." His brows rose as he got an idea, looking at Ryder as if for confirmation. "Hey! I know what you could—"

"That's no problem, Jed," Laura interrupted. "I'll be staying at the— Ouch! That hurt," she cried. Ryder was roughly applying a bandage to her knee, and he prevented her from hopping off the desk by his firm grasp on her calf.

"One more ought to do it," Ryder stated without apology, bending his head as he applied a bandage to her other knee.

She had the fleeting impression that Ryder had deliberately been rough when he applied the first bandage but dismissed the thought when she saw how carefully he applied the second, his fingers gentle as he pressed the tape down on her skin. "I'm staying at the Cliffs, Jed. If I leave you my keys, can you tow my car in and have it repaired? I could pick it up here later in the day."

"Sure thing," Jed reassured with reservations. "But it might be more than a day if I don't have the parts in stock."

"That's all right. I'm not going anywhere." Laura smiled. "I plan to live here." She wondered why both men were looking at her with such intent expressions and received part of the answer when Jed cocked a bushy gray brow and broke into a toothy grin.

"Say? Ain't you old Merrill Davis's granddaughter?" Jed asked, examining her face. "You sure have changed over the years you've been gone."

She gave him a warm smile that radiated like sunshine. "Yes, I am. Did you know my grandfather?" Digging in her purse, she removed her keys and handed them to Jed, glancing quickly at Ryder when she sensed that he was staring at her. She promptly turned away when she noted the grim set of his mouth, confused by the alarming intensity in his eyes.

"You sure have changed over the years since you've been gone," Jed said, smiling, "I was sure sorry to hear Merrill passed on." Jed began wiping his face to give her a better view of his features. "I'm Dan Canaly's pa. Danny went to school with you. Remember my boy?"

Without the layers of grease, Laura recognized her schoolmate's father even though she'd only met him a couple of times. They immediately launched into a conversation about his son and the local girl he'd married.

In the years since she'd left Mainport, the younger Canaly had gone into the lumber business; his wife, Sue, was now Tom Anderson's legal secretary. "Fine boy, that Tom," Jed remarked, unaware of Ryder's growing impatience with their conversation. "Didn't you and Tom once have a thing going? I seemed to recall he was your escort when you were voted homecoming queen your senior year."

Laura laughed, tossing back the thick blond mane of her hair as the memories of those pleasurable days returned to warm her. "That was a long time ago, Mr. Canaly. Tom's sister, Jill, was my best friend, and I guess Tom often got roped into being my date."

"As I remember it, he wasn't complaining." Jed folded his arms across his chest, beaming at her.

Laura was startled when a heavy hand descended on her shoulder. "I can take you out to the Cliffs." Ryder interrupted whatever else Jed was planning to say. "Are you ready to go?"

"I can't let you do that," Laura said firmly, but Ryder

was there to take her elbow when she gingerly slid down off the desk.

"That's where I'm heading, so you might as well come with me." Ryder insisted, ushering her toward the door.

"T'ain't no trouble 'bout your car," Jed called as she was hustled outside and assisted into the cab of the truck. Ryder shut the door with a loud slam, drowning Jed's parting comments as he waved at them from the doorway of the garage.

"You are the rudest man!" Laura waited until Ryder had started the engine before she told him what she thought of his highhandedness.

"You needed a ride, and I was on my way to the Cliffs," Ryder drawled. "I'm sure you were thoroughly enjoying that sentimental discussion of bygone years, but I don't have that kind of time to waste. I hadn't planned on spending the rest of my evening in Jed's garage."

Containing her curiosity about the slight southern accent she'd suddenly detected in his well-modulated voice, Laura assessed his short speech. It wasn't as if she and Jed had spent hours discussing people Ryder didn't know, but she realized it probably was boring for him. She decided it would be wiser to drop the subject. "I do appreciate all you've done," she told him, hoping her voice expressed more conviction than she felt.

"You're welcome." Ryder adjusted his long body behind the wheel, placing his arm along the edge of the open window and steering with one hand. "Like I said, we're both going to the same place."

"Why?"

"Why what?"

"Why are you going to the Cliffs?"

"Because that's where I'm staying." He gave her a penetrating sidelong glance. "You seem surprised."

Laura flushed, unsettled by his uncanny ability to read her mind. Since he wasn't dressed like the clientele that normally stayed at the Cliffs, she concluded he must be one of the "boat people" who docked at the marina and stayed overnight at the inn. "Do you own a boat?" she inquired.

He hesitated a moment before answering. "I guess you could say I own part interest in several boats." A wary expression came into his eyes, and he took a deep breath. "Haven't you guessed by now who I am?"

Laura's puzzled look told him that she had no idea what he was talking about. "I'm sorry?"

"Ryder Bantel." Seeing her contemplative frown, he elaborated. "Wilson R. Bantel . . ."

"You're the man who wants to buy the Cliffs?" Laura's shocked eyes traveled to his face, the amber flecks in their depths igniting like sparks.

"I've made an offer, yes." Ryder didn't sound as if he wished to discuss the matter further, saying, "We'll have plenty of time to talk about that later on."

"Why are you suddenly telling me who you are?" Laura questioned shortly. "You were certainly reluctant to do so earlier when you found out my name."

"You could say I was as surprised as you," Ryder admitted, shrugging his shoulders. "I knew you were coming, but you didn't inform anyone exactly when. I suppose I should have told you right off who I was, but you weren't in the best of moods, and I didn't want to make matters worse. Tom told me you'd only been recently informed that I was the manager and that you wouldn't be pleased having an outsider overseeing the place. Maybe I wanted to clean up and make a better impression on you when we met."

"Forgive me for doubting you, Mr. Bantel," Laura said disdainfully, "but you don't strike me as a man who cares what kind of impression he makes."

He didn't respond to that verbally, but the slight upward tilt at the corners of his mouth told her she was right in her estimation.

"You've called me Ryder up until now." He grinned at her. "Why don't we keep things informal." Taking her silence as agreement, he went on. "Let's not get into anything tonight, Laura. You look like all you're up to right now is a hot bath and a good night's sleep."

"How I look doesn't matter, Mr . . . uh . . . Ryder." Laura bristled. "It seems a perfectly good time to tell you that I won't be selling."

"You can make up your mind about things after you've talked everything over with your attorney."

Laura didn't like the feeling that he was patronizing her, and the stubborn thrust of her chin told him so. "Tom's house is at the end of this road. Let's stop and get this settled tonight. Perhaps then you'll realize I mean what I say."

Ryder laughed, a loud rumble that reverberated inside the enclosed cab. "Look at yourself. Your attorney'll probably think you've just been mugged. Even worse, he might think you and I have—"

"Tom won't think anything of the kind." Laura wouldn't let him finish. "This is more important to me than worrying if every hair on my head is in place."

"You've got more than just a hair out of place, honey," Ryder declared outrageously. "Good ol' Tom might really wonder what went on out there on the road. His homecoming queen looks like she's just had a nice roll in the mud. Your hair's all messed up. Your blouse is all wet, and it's halfway undone. I can see all the way to your—"

"Stop it!" Laura exclaimed furiously, horrified when she looked down and discovered he was right. Crossing her arms defensively over her chest, she glared at him until he relented and stared straight ahead through the windshield, giving her the chance to rebutton her blouse. Once she was sure the small buttons wouldn't come loose again, she launched into an attack of her own. "Speaking of appearances, what is the interim manager of the Cliffs and a supposedly viable buyer doing dressed up like a farmer and driving this wreck of a truck?"

Refusing to be baited, Ryder stated calmly, "The clothes and the truck fit the job I've been doing. I found some old wicker furniture in a storage shed and used the truck to take them to a retired couple I found living in Toledo who specialize in wicker repair and upholstery. I'm on my way back from there."

"And who gave you permission to take that kind of job on yourself?" Laura knew she was being petty, but he acted as if he owned the place instead of being appointed manager in her stead. She saw that he was having difficulty maintaining his placid expression and for some perverse reason, pressed the point. "Who gave you the right to rummage through Davis belongings and decide for yourself that they needed repair? What if I refuse to pay for the work? Then where will you be?"

"Hold on there, Laura." Ryder's voice went soft,

each word a gentle rasp that raised the tiny hairs at the nape of her neck. "When Merrill made me manager, he gave me the right to make those kind of decisions. He believed in me, and you'll just have to accept that."

"We'll see about that," Laura said tersely, unnerved by his quiet tone. Again, she took note of the slight drawl in his voice, beginning to realize that he acquired the melodious speech pattern whenever he was angry. Her determination to dismiss Ryder at the earliest opportunity was steadily increasing, aware that she was dealing with a man who could be dangerous to her in ways she didn't even want to think about. Silently, she recalled the old furniture that had been piled in the shed, admitting to herself that she'd thought it a waste to allow it to fall into further decay. She'd planned to investigate the storage sheds on the place and make sure nothing was stored that could be refurbished and put to good use, but she resented Ryder for taking matters into his own hands without consulting her. After all, she was the owner, and he was . . . he was her employee! But perhaps her grandfather had somehow guaranteed Ryder's job; perhaps that was the complication that had developed since the reading of the will.

"I'm scheduled to meet with my attorney tomorrow." Laura attempted to match his restraint. "I'll then know the extent of my control, so I suggest you stop any other plans you may have made that might require my approval."

There was a long tension-filled silence; then Ryder said quietly, in the dangerous tone that indicated his acute annoyance, "Don't worry; if anything I do requires your approval, I'll make sure I get it."

"Thank you." Laura was unsure whether or not

she'd won the point but didn't dare push her luck any further, especially when she noticed the stony expression on Ryder's face. The truck passed Tom Anderson's house, and neither one of them said a word as Ryder drove on.

After that, a strained hush descended that lasted all the way to their destination. Glad that her imposing companion appeared to need his full concentration to steer his truck around the curves in the road, Laura leaned her head back on the cool vinyl upholstery and took a calming breath of the lake-scented air. As the truck lumbered along the winding lake's edge toward the peninsula and the Cliffs, she realized just how much she'd missed the smell of the water, the cool evening breezes off the lake, and the sound of lapping waves on the shore. Her apartment in Chicago and the school where she had taught were not close to the lake, and though she had often driven to Lake Michigan and walked along its edge, it wasn't the same as living near the water and waking up to the familiar sounds and smells every day.

They drove along the rocky cliffs, the road beginning a steady incline, hugging the fern-strewn rocks on one side and the sharp drop to the lake on the other. A few stars twinkled overhead, but the thin sliver of moon cast only a faint sheen of light across the lake's undulating surface. She gazed out across the dark water, thinking the brooding black rollers washing the shore matched her present mood. Since running into Ryder Bantel, everything that had been so clear to her before seemed unsettled. There was nothing he'd said that should've made her feel that way, but she sensed an undercurrent beneath every word he had spoken, and she didn't trust him. He didn't behave like a man who was about to lose his job, who was not going to be kept on even as a hotel management consultant, if the owner had anything to say about it.

A massive limestone post at each side of the drive signaled that they were about to enter through the gates to the Cliffs. A brass plate attached to the left post bore the name of her great-great-grandfather and the date 1872. A shiver of grief stabbed her like a knife as she thought about the generations of Davises that had once occupied the property. She was the last living member of the family. Her children would grow up there, and their children after them. They might not carry the Davis name, but they'd have Davis blood, and she had no intention of giving up their heritage. Ryder would soon find out that she wouldn't consider his offer no matter what price he presented to induce her to sell.

For generations, the Cliffs had served as the Davis family home, but after the Great Depression, Merrill Davis had converted the grand old house into an inn that expressly catered to families during the summer tourist season. Its location at the tip of a small, picturesque peninsula provided, in addition to a spectacular view, ready access to Lake Erie. A small pier had been expanded to a marina, and boat owners could dock their boats and spend a pleasant night in the comfortable inn. The Cliffs maintained a medium-sized cabin cruiser that was used to ferry guests across the lakes to the islands and for fishing, while several smaller craft were kept for water-skiing. Over the years, the inn had provided the Davis family with a comfortable and steady income, and Laura planned to uphold that tradition.

"We're home, Laura." Ryder's voice broke the silence of her intense thoughts.

"I'm home," she corrected pointedly, and didn't wait for him before stepping out of the truck and walking across the stone pathway that led to the small covered porch in front of her house.

3

~~~~~~~~~~~~

A thick wall of pine and several yards of rolling lawn separated the Davis family home from the inn. Taking a brief glance through the fragrant boughs, Laura was reassured by the filtered light, which told her the inn was enjoying a high rate of occupancy. Very happy that she'd soon be minus Ryder's unsettling company, she inserted her key and entered the house. As she switched on the foyer light, she heard Ryder coming up behind her. She assumed he would deposit her luggage, then go over to the inn, where he probably occupied one of the rooms. Instead, he brushed right past her and strode down the hall toward the stairs leading to the four bedrooms on the second floor. He seemed to know his way around the house, and Laura was still standing by the open door when, a few moments later, he walked back down the hall and closed it for her.

"Are you planning on standing by the door all night, or would you rather come and sit down in the living room?" Ryder asked, not waiting to hear her answer as he walked into the room and began turning on the lights.

"Mr. Bantel," Laura began, but he was already heading for the kitchen and didn't let her complete her sentence.

He called back over his shoulder, "The name's Ryder. Would you like coffee or something stronger? I'm having a scotch. I'll be back with some ice in a minute."

He was actually playing host in her home! All she wanted to do was get rid of him, then take a bath and crawl into bed. Every inch of her body yearned for a hot tub of water to rinse away the dirt and perspiration from her aching muscles. She couldn't do that until he'd left, and it certainly didn't look as if he intended to leave very soon.

Attempting to extricate herself gracefully from his unwanted company, she called out, "That won't be necessary, thank you. It was kind of you to bring my luggage all the way upstairs, but now you can be on your way. I'm really tired and would like to lock up the house and go to bed."

"Suit yourself." Ryder seemed not to have understood her dismissal, for he strode back into the living room and over to the liquor cabinet. He clinked a few ice cubes into his glass, then leisurely poured himself a drink before turning back to her. "Are you sure you wouldn't like to join me in a drink first? It's been quite a night. There's some brandy in here. It might help you sleep."

He lowered himself to the comfortable easy chair that

stood beside the large limestone fireplace dominating one end of the room. Gesturing with his glass to the liquor cabinet, he continued. "Please help yourself to whatever you'd like, but stop standing at the door as if you've taken root. You're making me uncomfortable."

"I'm making you uncomfortable!" Laura exploded, unconsciously obeying his suggestion by charging into the room. "That's an understatement! This is my house, and you're the one who's making himself right at home." When Ryder didn't respond to her accusation, Laura persisted. "You're acting like you belong here."

"I do," Ryder announced calmly, his storm-swept eyes the only indication that he wasn't as relaxed as he sounded.

"You live here?" Laura couldn't believe her ears. He was manager, not owner of the Cliffs, and it was an ideal time to remind him of the differences in their positions. Authoritatively, she ordered, "Well, you can't stay in my house now that I've come home. I suggest you make arrangements for a room at the inn. You can use the phone if you'd rather not go across until you've been assigned a vacancy."

Thinking the matter had been settled, Laura was not prepared for Ryder's brisk rejoinder. "I can't do that because every room in the place is booked." His control finally wavered when he saw that she wouldn't accept that excuse. A muscle pulsed in his cheek as he swore. "I'll be damned if I'll sleep on the floor in the office when there's a perfectly good bed upstairs with nobody in it. Four beds!" he added as if provoked by the unrelenting shards of amber in her gray eyes.

Exasperated that she had not yet won her case, Laura grudgingly sat down on the edge of a small straight-backed chair, unconsciously scowling as she scratched at one of the irritating red welts on her arm. Very aware of her muddied clothing, she imagined what her grandmother might have said to her if she'd caught her sitting on the living-room furniture in dirty clothes. She was growing more and more impatient with the man who was keeping her from her bath. "You must see that's not possible. You'll have to move over to the inn."

He sighed deeply, then burst out, "Look, Laura, your grandfather invited me to move in here when he appointed me manager. I'm sorry he died before he could explain our business arrangement to you, but I'm not going anywhere tonight except upstairs to bed."

They were deadlocked, and Laura couldn't think of a single thing to say that wouldn't make her sound like a straight-laced autocrat from a previous century. Her knees were beginning to throb, and she clenched and unclenched her hands in an effort to keep from screaming her frustration at the man sprawled nonchalantly in her grandfather's chair, showing no signs of moving.

It had been a long, hot drive from Chicago, and she was exhausted. The fight went out of her, and she arched her neck, massaging the stiff muscles at her nape with her battered hands.

Ryder was watching her closely, noting the fatigue etched on her classically lovely face. Her homecoming had certainly complicated matters. When her trunks and boxes had arrived earlier in the week, he'd been completely surprised and had hoped they heralded an upcoming vacation, but she had told Jed she'd come back for good. Knowing his timing couldn't have been worse, he broached the subject, anyway. "Neither your grandfather nor I considered that you'd want to come back here for any great length of time. School starts up again in a couple of weeks, so you'll have to be going back to teaching, won't you?"

Laura couldn't misinterpret the hopefulness in his question or resist stating bluntly, "I resigned from teaching. I intend to make this my home and manage the inn myself. Since my grandfather told you that I was a teacher, I'm surprised he didn't also tell you I was considering making a change."

He would have probed that more deeply, but she didn't look up to any more serious discussion tonight. He admired her tenacious spirit and couldn't help but respect her for resolutely challenging his position, although clearly dead on her feet. At the moment, she greatly resembled her late grandparent, who had the same stubborn thrust to his chin, but on Laura the trait was softened by a delicate facial structure, provocative gray eyes, and a pair of soft lips that almost begged to be kissed. Knowing it was the last thing she'd allow, he resisted the strong urge he felt to cross the room, scoop her up in his arms, and carry her up the stairs to bed. Realizing it was her vulnerability and endearingly tousled beauty that was intriguing him, he reminded himself to remain objective. "It's pointless to get into this now. We're both wiped out. Let's declare a truce until after the meeting tomorrow. Since we're both adults, I think we can stay under the same roof for one night without creating any more problems."

"Before tonight, I wasn't aware I had any problems," Laura disclosed caustically. "Someone should have warned me."

Shrugging, Ryder got up from the chair and wearily retraced his steps to the liquor cabinet, then poured himself another measure of scotch over the melting ice in his glass. "Why don't you take the bathroom first. I'm going to stay down here and finish this drink, then read the paper."

"How gracious of you," Laura finally muttered sarcastically. For tonight, anyway, she knew she was beaten, and she rose from her chair, making an awkward start for the stairs. Moving slowly to accommodate the stiff muscles in her legs, she reached the bottom step. Her hand clinging to the rail, she turned back for her final shot. "I hope you haven't taken over the master bedroom like you seem to have taken over everything else. I will draw the line at that."

She knew she sounded spiteful but didn't care. She wanted him to know that she looked on him as an usurper who had grossly overstepped his bounds. "Or my room, Ryder? Perhaps you thought it appropriate to move in there."

When she got no response, she started up the stairs, but halted when she heard Ryder's deep laugh. Turning to look down, she found him lounging against the living-room door frame, one knee bent so his foot could rest against the baseboard, his shoulders clearly defined against the dark wood. His blue eyes were twinkling like summer stars, the dimples in his cheeks widening the amused smile that pulled at his mouth. "I'll give you credit; even as tired as you are, your tongue is still sharp." He lifted his glass in a mocking salute. "Canopied beds and lace curtains aren't my style, and regardless of your opinion of me, your grandfather's room seemed entirely too personal. You'll find your luggage in your old room and me in the first room at the top of the stairs."

Flushing, Laura tore her eyes away from him and hurried the rest of the way up the stairs, needing the sanctuary of her bedroom for more reasons than rest. Although she didn't understand it, Ryder had the ability to scatter her emotions like sand on a wind-swept beach, and she didn't like it at all.

Slamming the door shut behind her, Laura stripped out of her soiled clothes and tossed them into the hamper next to her closet. Out of long habit, she opened the closet door, surprised and delighted when she found that all of the belongings she'd shipped were hanging inside, including her short terry robe.

Smiling, she lifted the robe off its hook on the door, thinking that Sophie Morrison had kindly unpacked her trunks and put everything away for her, the same way she'd always done whenever Laura had come home from college or for a vacation. Sophie and her husband, Will, had worked at the Cliffs longer than Laura had lived, and she felt as close to them as if they were an additional set of grandparents. Sophie had once been the head of housekeeping at the inn, and her husband had been in charge of the boat marina and grounds. In recent years, the elderly couple had been gradually relieved of their duties until Sophie had served only as Gramps' housekeeper. Will spent the majority of his time keeping the boats at the dock in working order. The couple lived in their own cottage, which Merrill Davis had built for them, at the far corner of the property, overlooking the lake. To Laura, the Morrisons were an extension of her family, another set of grand parents who had loved her since she was a little girl.

Grabbing her cosmetic bag from the travel case, Laura ventured back out of the room and down the hall. The sight that greeted her when she entered the bathroom and caught a good look at herself in the mirror over the sink had her talking out loud to her outlandish reflection. "My God, Laura. You are some sight. No wonder that damned squatter couldn't keep from laughing at you."

There was a wide streak of mud across her forehead, nose, and one cheek. Her hair hung in wild, limp strands about her face, and there were unbecoming dark shadows under both eyes. Taking immediate action, she applied a liberal amount of cleansing cream to her face and rinsed it off with warm water. Seeing a definite improvement, she rummaged in her bag for her hairbrush and set to work. A vigorous brushing restored some of the gold luster to her hair, but it definitely needed to be washed. She was too tired to dry the thick mass of blond curls that night, so she pinned it up on the top of her head and walked into the divided bathroom to ready the tub.

The deep claw-foot tub looked totally incongruous among the other more modern fixtures in the bathroom but had never looked more welcome. Laura turned on the ornate spigots and sprinkled a handful of fragrant bubble bath into the warm water. Swishing her hand to disperse the crystals, she thought back to the time her grandfather had presented the beautiful old tub to her grandmother. Gram had enjoyed long, luxurious baths and had complained for years about the shallow modern tub that had been installed when the house had been remodeled earlier. Gramps had preferred showers, so when he finally decided to give in to his wife's wishes, he'd built a small separate stall for himself on one side and converted a walk-in closet into grandma's "soaking room" on the other. The result was an unorthodox three-room bath, but it suited the Davis family life style. Gram had been able to soak in the tub for as long as she wished without inconveniencing anyone else.

Laura slipped out of her robe and sank gratefully into the soothing water. Leaning back, she let the warmth soak into her aching muscles and take the sting from the mosquito bites that dotted her arms and legs. The strain of the long drive, coupled with the disastrous events on the road, had taken their toll, and she closed her eyes. Her mind drifted aimlessly as she fell asleep, not waking until the water turned cold and the bubbles had fizzed out on the flat surface.

Hoping she wouldn't catch cold on top of everything else, she quickly climbed out of the tub and vigorously toweled herself dry. Slipping into her robe, she stepped into the other room, but froze in alarm when she saw Ryder standing before the long vanity.

Clad in nothing but a pair of blue pajama bottoms, he was fresh from the shower. A white towel was slung around his neck, and he was vigorously brushing his teeth. It was only a matter of time before he spotted her standing in the doorway between rooms, but she delayed the inevitable confrontation by taking a step back so he wouldn't see her reflection in the mirror.

Involuntarily, her gaze flickered over the broad strength of his bronzed back, down to the tapered waist, tight buttocks, and long, powerful legs; from behind, he was intriguingly magnificent. Then she shifted her position—she couldn't help herself—until she gained a frontal view, reflected to her from the mirror. Well-developed pectoral muscles gleamed across his chest; droplets of water sparkled in the curling dark hair that stretched between his flat nipples, then diminished to an alluring line that disappeared down below his waist. The wide elastic band of his pajamas hung loosely about his slim hips, and she had difficulty pulling her eyes away from his burnished smooth skin. It was a pleasure to look at him, and Laura didn't realize he was aware of her intimate inspection until he dropped his toothbrush into his shaving kit and turned around to face her.

"Sorry, Laura. I didn't know you were in there." But he didn't look very sorry as he examined the telltale pink of her cheeks, his sparkling blue eyes disclosing that he had been aware of her thorough inspection of him all along. "I assumed you'd have tucked yourself safely under that canopy long ago. It's been over an hour since you came up."

As Laura stood there trying to think of something to say, Ryder's amused blue eyes dropped pointedly to the gaping front of her terry robe, which revealed the shadowed outline of her breasts, then lower, to assess the long, shapely legs that were exposed below the hem. Laura could feel his heated perusal as clearly as if he were touching her and immediately pulled together the edges of her robe, tightening the sash.

Wishing she'd worn her floor-length bathrobe instead of the short one that barely covered her bottom, she stammered, "I . . . I didn't hear you come in. I'm sorry I took so long. I must have fallen asleep in the tub." She edged toward the door but couldn't escape the room without asking him to move, and he didn't look inclined to give way.

"You're really beautiful without all that mud on your face," he murmured huskily, continuing his close study as if he were seeing her for the first time. He took one step toward her, then another, advancing slowly until she was trapped against the wall. "I don't think any

44

man in his right mind could resist taking advantage of this situation."

"Ryder," she warned anxiously, but when she defiantly lifted her chin, his head was already descending, and his lips closed over her startled mouth. His hands curved around her shoulders, and he pulled her against the hard masculine planes she had just admired so much in the mirror. His thighs tingled against her bare legs, and whether it was from exhaustion or a purely physical response, she leaned closer. Breathing in the fresh soapy smell of him, she tasted the light mint flavor of his breath and couldn't deny that it felt wonderful to be kissed. His mouth moved languidly, lightly, then hardened with determined hunger as she gave into the pleasurable sensation and willingly parted her lips. Instantly, he pulled her into better contact, and she responded by sliding her hands around his waist, splaying her fingers across the warm, damp skin of his back.

Even knowing that the two of them had placed themselves on opposite sides of some invisible fence, Laura still couldn't prevent herself from enjoying his embrace. Opening her lips for the gentle intrusion of his tongue, she gained intense satisfaction in the sound of his aroused growl as his hands wandered down her shoulders to her back, exploring her curves through the rough terry of her robe. It was only when his warm fingers began working to release her sash that some shred of common sense took hold. She let go of him and clutched at his wrists, pushing his hands away from the front of her robe as she stiffened in his arms.

Initially, Ryder seemed reluctant to accept her sudden rejection, but then he lifted his lips away from hers and took a slight step backward. Still not entirely willing to accept her decision, he kept her trapped by placing one arm on each side of her body, pressing his hands flat against the wall.

Angry with herself for responding so completely to his kiss, she stared at him in mute dismay. "Let go of me," she ordered, upset by the piquant huskiness evident in her voice.

By his disturbed breathing, she could tell that he'd been as fully aroused as she, so his apology came as a dampening shock. "I shouldn't have let this happen." He lifted one hand and raked it through his damp black hair, then dropped his other arm and stepped aside. "Call it a mental—" He appeared to have thought of a more plausible excuse. "No, consider it your thanks to me for being a Good Samaritan."

"Next time, I'll offer you cash," Laura said angrily, then whirled away from him and out the door. He'd had little difficulty making their passionate encounter seem meaningless, but she'd never felt more shaken, and his attempt to toss it off as payment for his earlier assistance rankled.

"Hey!" he called after her, but she could hear the amused lilt in his voice and didn't pause in her flight down the hall. Unfortunately, his booming shout followed her into the sanctuary of her bedroom and reached her as she leaned back against the door. "Your brand of gratitude was greatly appreciated. I never said I didn't enjoy every second of it."

"Oh!" Laura gasped, thoroughly enraged. Without thinking, she kicked the wood door with her bare foot, wishing it were him. "The jerk," she moaned, hopping on one foot to the bed so she could sit down and nurse her bruised toes. "It'll never happen again," she promised between her teeth, trying to rid herself of the feel of his muscular body pressed intimately against hers and the intoxicating smell of him that still pervaded her nostrils. Raising trembling finger tips to her swollen lips, she tried to erase his taste, ashamed of how easy she'd made it for him to delve into her mouth.

She almost jumped off the bed when she heard his footsteps in the hall, only releasing her pent-up breath when they passed by her room and entered the guest room. At the sound of his door closing, she got under the covers of her bed, curling up into a tight ball beneath the fluffy eyelet comforter. Sleep was a long time coming, and even then her dreams were haunted by images of his handsome face bending closer and closer, his blue eyes hypnotizing her before he laid claim to her lips again and again.

4

Laura awoke the next morning to the sound of rain pelting against the glass panes of her bedroom window. She could hear the pounding waves crashing against the rocky shore line only a few yards away and nestled deeper into the warmth of her bed. It was not the change in the weather that made her shudder but her instantaneous recall of the previous night. She was still wearing her short terry robe, and as she tightened the sash, she remembered every detail of Ryder's embrace. Why had she responded to him so easily? The man had been a thorn in her side since she'd first set eyes on him and his broken-down truck, and he would probably cause her more trouble in the future, but she'd thoroughly enjoyed being in his arms. Comforting herself with the thought that she'd soon be able to get rid of him, she forced herself to think of other things.

Propping herself up against the pillows, her eyes

wandered around the room; it had not changed since she was a little girl. All the events of the past month came flooding back into her mind, and she was overcome by a great sense of loss. The smell of bacon drifting upstairs from the big old kitchen tantalized her nostrils, and she half expected Gram to call her down to breakfast at any moment. She could almost hear Grandfather Merrill's cheery "Good-morning, princess" floating musically from the other side of her door. She gave herself a small shake, knowing that those one-time regular occurrences would never happen again; they were only cherished memories.

Throwing back the coverlet, she jumped out of bed and crossed the room to her closet. Keeping in mind her afternoon appointment with Tom Anderson, she studied the possibilities of what to wear. Since Ryder Bantel would be present, she was determined to look her best. So far, Ryder had only seen her muddied, disheveled, or almost naked from her bath. She planned to wear something that would project an image of cool sophistication and convince him she was a serious businesswoman, serious about dismissing him. She could hardly blame him for questioning her suitability as manager of the Cliffs in the light of the miserable showing she'd made the previous night, but it was a new day, and she was going to be ready for him.

Deciding that she'd wear a navy gabardine skirt and a crisp, tailored white blouse, she extracted her long robe from the closet and proceeded to the bathroom to wash her hair. After blowing it dry, she returned to her bedroom, got dressed, and began applying her makeup. She brushed the unruly tumble of golden curls back from her face and neatly secured its length with a tortoise-shell clasp at the nape of her neck. Satisfied with her appearance, she slipped a wide gold bracelet on each wrist, fitted small matching hoops in her ears, then slid her feet into a pair of navy heels. She gave herself a final glance in the cheval mirror that stood in one corner of her room, smiling at the self-assured-looking woman reflected there who could easily be accepted as the owner of a small inn.

Anxious to see Sophie, she hurriedly descended the stairs and walked down the long hall to the kitchen. Pushing open the swinging door, she delivered the morning greeting she'd always made to announce her arrival for breakfast. "Your golden girl is starving, Sophie. What have you got?"

"Anything you'd like . . . golden girl." Ryder's voice replaced the one she'd been expecting, and it was his aproned form that occupied Sophie's accustomed place in front of the stove.

Cursing herself for allowing him to catch her unprepared yet again, Laura strove to appear casual as she entered the room. "I thought you were Sophie," she admitted, feeling like an idiot for calling herself by the affectionate nickname her family had given her years before.

"You look like you've had a good night's sleep," Ryder said, his bold eyes taking in every inch of her as she walked to the counter and poured herself a cup of coffee. "Take a seat. I've made eggs ranchero to go with the bacon. I thought I'd have to come upstairs and wake you so you wouldn't miss out on tasting my specialty."

Not wanting to think about what it would've been like to have him coax her out of bed, Laura assessed the ludicrous image he presented in Sophie's bright calico apron. Even though the feminine garment covered a light beige sweater and dark brown cords, he had tied the apron strings in a large flamboyant bow behind his waist, and one lacy yellow ruffle was constantly slipping off one shoulder. Seemingly oblivious to how ridiculous he looked, he kept readjusting the ruffle as he brought several dishes out of the oven.

Laura was bolted to the spot, watching in fascination as he arranged several pecan rolls on a plate, then expertly juggled the other dishes into position on his arm as he carried them to the table. He waved at her to join him, pointing out that the table had been set for two, but when she showed no inclination toward moving, he snapped his fingers to bring her out of her bemused state. "Don't you want to test my culinary talents? I thought you said you were starving."

Laura swiftly crossed to the table and took the chair opposite his. "But where's Sophie? I thought she'd be here this morning."

"There was no need to bother her with breakfast. I've been taking care of myself for years and can cook a decent meal. You can run across to see her after we eat. I told her you were sleeping in late this morning."

Glancing at the clock on the wall over the door, Laura's brows rose. "It's only eight, not eleven."

"I've been up since six," he mumbled while taking a large bite of a homemade roll. "I'm addicted to Sophie's baking. She sends these over all the time, so help yourself. My, how that woman spoils me."

"She's been spoiling me for years," Laura pointed out, then wished she hadn't, for it made her sound as if she were jealous of him, and she had no reason to be. Attempting to rectify that impression, she smoothly continued. "I'd like to be polite about this, Ryder. I

51

don't think I've made my position clear. I intend to take over as man—"

"Don't talk business before breakfast; it's uncivilized," he interrupted, and heaped her plate with a mound of spicy eggs and a hearty rasher of bacon.

"I don't normally eat this big a breakfast," she said, frowning down at the pile of food on her plate. "This is too much."

"That's not how it sounded when you thought Sophie was doing the cooking," he reminded her. "Every 'golden girl' needs a good breakfast."

It was disconcerting to find him studying her mouth as she lifted her fork. "Don't call me that," she ordered, hoping he'd stop staring at her, but her rude demand only intensified his inquiring gaze.

"It certainly fits," he said blandly, but she had the annoying impression he felt the nickname suited her for an entirely different reason than the one that had inspired it.

"My family called me that because of my hair," she began, pushing her food around on her plate. "But I don't like anyone else using that nickname."

"Okay." He shrugged and returned his attention to his meal.

Thinking she'd be better off eating than attempting any further conversation with him, she tasted the eggs. They were delicious, and the more she ate, the more she realized how hungry she actually was. Her body certainly could use a good supply of fuel in order to match wits with the man across the table.

After eating every morsel he had placed on her plate, she leaned back and gave a replete sigh. "My compliments to the chef," she said, holding out her cup as

Ryder came back to the table with the coffeepot. "I've enjoyed being waited on."

A small furrow developed between his brows, but it was quickly gone as he took his seat. "I learned how to cook in the army. As it happens, I once waited tables, so that comes easily, too."

"From a lowly waiter to a representative of a management consulting firm. You've come a long way, haven't you?"

Although Laura hadn't meant anything snide by the question, Ryder took offense. "Meaning?"

Startled by the change in tone signaling his anger, Laura took a sip of coffee before saying soothingly, "Meaning you've come up in the world. Aren't you proud of how much you've accomplished?"

There was a lengthy pause before he answered. "Yes, I'm damned proud. I'm not a representative of the firm, Laura. I own it and worked long and hard to make it one of the most respected companies going." He placed unnecessary stress on the words "long" and "hard," and Laura didn't like what he was implying. There was something else about his statement that bothered her, but she didn't waste any time trying to figure out what it was, responding instead to his unsubtle jibe.

"And you don't think I've worked hard enough to deserve ownership of this place?" she inquired bitingly. "I've worked here every summer since I was nine years old."

"Doing what? Greeting all the tourists? Giving directions to the dock? We're not talking about a part-time summer job to keep you from getting bored, Laura. We're talking about a demanding occupation that doesn't end when you find you'd rather do something else."

"I was a teacher." Laura could feel the blood rushing to her cheeks at his unfair attack. "If anything can be demanding, it's spending an entire day with thirty-five children who don't want to learn anything but the best ways to skip school."

"And you quit," Ryder declared triumphantly, making her more angry than she'd ever been in her life. "Did the going get too tough for you?"

Fighting for control, Laura forced the cold words through her teeth. "I gave it up for this, Ryder. Why I did is none of your business. Since I'm here now, your services are no longer required. Why don't you send me a bill. I'd be happy to pay it if it will speed up your departure."

His eyes had never looked more intensely blue as they cut into her face. Refusing to cower beneath his glare, she had no idea that the amber flecks in her own eyes had blazed to life and were having the same effect on him as they'd had the previous day. Not understanding why he suddenly changed tactics, she didn't know what to reply when he grinned at her, saying, "I'll overlook that last remark. I don't think you'll be so anxious to be rid of me when you've heard all the facts."

He pushed his chair away from the table and stood up. "In the meantime, I've got a lot of work to do."

Striding across the brick-patterned linoleum, he lifted a rain slicker off a hook by the door and pulled it over his head. "To keep things fair, since I made breakfast, you should—"

"You expect me to clean up?" Dubiously, she looked toward the stack of dirty pots and pans he'd piled in the sink, the number of utensils lying on the stove, and the various bowls and dishes cluttered on the counter.

"Very kind of you." He opened the door, pausing before he stepped outside into the rain. "One of us has to get on with the business of running this place, and since you haven't been brought up to date, that's me. By the way, I've relieved Sophie from cooking duty here at the house. She's not as strong as she used to be. Later, we'll figure out what to do about our meals. See you later."

He was gone before Laura could form an appropriate reply, and she was left faced with a messy kitchen and the feeling it was punishment for expecting someone else to wait on her. Well, she hadn't asked him to make her breakfast, and he didn't have to sound as if she were taking advantage of an old woman's generosity. Besides, if anyone should have told Sophie she no longer had to make meals, it should have been her, not Ryder. At least cleaning up would kill some time, and she could hardly wait until her meeting with Tom. It was going to give her a great deal of pleasure to fire Ryder Bantel immediately thereafter. Feeling like a prisoner unfairly sentenced to hard labor, she lifted Sophie's apron off the back of Ryder's chair and put it on. "The jury's still out on your case, Ryder." She flung the words at the closed kitchen door, then marched to the sink and turned the water on full force. "But after two o'clock, I'll be the judge, and I'll be the one making changes and delivering orders around here."

Ryder maneuvered along the puddle-obstructed walkway between the family house and the inn and ducked inside the service door. His usual jocular bantering with the kitchen staff was replaced by a barely genial smile and a curt wave of his hand as he hastily made his way past the grill and down the hall leading to the manager's office. Once inside, he hung up his dripping slicker and slumped into the heavy arm chair behind the wide scarred desk.

Damn! Why did Laura Davis have to show up, and why did she have to be so attractive? It wasn't the first time he'd posed the question to himself, and he was angrily certain it wouldn't be the last. He'd known she was a pretty girl from the photos sprinkled throughout the house and Merrill's office, but the pictures didn't do justice to the woman she'd become. Rather than the superficial blonde he'd expected, she was a vibrantly alive and intelligent woman. With her tawny wild mane of hair and gold-flecked eyes, she conveyed a feline strength. Prepared for a domesticated gold kitten, he found himself dealing with an untamed lioness made of gilded steel.

Kissing her the night before had been a mistake, for the powerful emotions she'd aroused in him would only complicate the issue between them. He smacked one fist into the open palm of his hand and stared around the room. If only Merrill had lived long enough to explain their agreement to his granddaughter, the whole miserable mess could have been avoided. Or would it? Had Merrill underestimated Laura's love of the Cliffs? She was a Davis, and from her attitude the previous night and that morning, she meant to assert her rights as the last living member of the family.

There was no doubt that Laura considered him an outsider, and Ryder cringed, knowing she hoped she'd soon be rid of him, guiltily aware it wouldn't be that simple for either of them. It was true that she had been born there, and it was understandable that she'd want to carry on the family tradition, but he loved the place, too, and had convinced Merrill that he had the know-how to turn the inn into a thriving, modern business.

Leaning back in his chair, his mind traveled back to the first time he'd viewed the Cliffs at the beginning of the summer. He had reluctantly agreed to contact Merrill Davis on his way back from a business trip to Canada and had planned to look over the place during the short break he had between jobs. The small lake-shore inn had turned out to be so peaceful and quiet, something he'd badly needed at the time, that he'd booked a room for an entire week. Unbelievably, he'd enjoyed his stay so much that he hadn't wanted to leave and surprised himself by booking in again. Feeling an urge to stay in one place was a startlingly new experience for him, and he spent the time re-evaluating his life style.

For years, he'd worked night and day to build his consulting firm, and he'd been more successful than he'd ever hoped. When the work had become more than he could handle by himself, he'd expanded his staff, but it was his presence that the hotel owners wanted on the job, and he was the one who flew from city to city, living out of a suitcase, never spending enough time in any one place to call it home.

The expensive apartment he rented in New York was supposed to be his private hideaway; instead, it had turned out to be an exquisitely decorated showplace where he slept between trips. It wasn't until he'd arrived at the Cliffs that he'd realized he had no roots or even that he wanted any.

For almost twenty years, he'd lived without a family,

and he'd done a fine job of convincing himself he didn't need anyone. After all, what had his parents ever done for him but work him to exhaustion from dawn to dusk on that miserable section of Georgia land his father had called a farm? He'd never forgotten his eighteenth birthday, when he'd come in after working all day in the field to find that his/chair had been removed from the kitchen table. Like his brother before him, he'd been told he was no longer a child but a man and it was high time he took off on his own, that they were no longer willing to stretch their meager earnings to include him. He'd left that very night, too proud to ask for more time to decide what to do with himself and disgusted with himself for naively believing it wouldn't be the same for him as it had been for his older brother, Ron, who'd left home years before. He'd run into Ron one day a few years back, but they'd had nothing in common, and Ryder doubted he'd ever see his brother again.

A week after he'd left home, the local recruiter had convinced him that the army would teach him all he'd need to know to make a success of himself; down to his last fifty cents, he'd enlisted. While in the service, he'd traveled the world, took some college courses, and after his tour, finished school on the G.I. Bill. His first job was in a small hotel in Pennsylvania where he'd hired on as a waiter, but the owners soon discovered he had some good ideas for turning a profit and let him implement some of them. It wasn't long before he was able to move on to another, larger hotel, then another, until he'd established his reputation and was being approached for advice. Soon after, he'd started his own firm and had since had the opportunity to prove his theories over and over again.

All of which had eventually led him to the Cliffs. Merrill Davis had asked him to come take a look, but instead of offering his professional advice, then moving on to another challenge, he'd wanted to stay and conquer the problems himself. He'd envisioned expansion and restoration and discovered those same dreams were shared by Merrill. A close friendship swiftly developed between them, and from it sprang the agreement that would soon bring matters to a head between him and Merrill's granddaughter.

Ryder glanced across the room to the simply framed photos that covered the wall. A little-girl Laura smiled back at him, proudly holding up a Lake Erie pickerel. Another picture showed a teenaged Laura attired in a short pleated skirt and a letter sweater, holding a pompon in her hand as she led a cheer for her high school football team. Laura being crowned homecoming queen, high school graduation—all of the pictures depicted highlights in the life of Merrill's "pride and joy."

"Damn it," Ryder swore, "it's my office." He couldn't recall one similar photograph being taken of him in his life; nor could he stand looking any longer at the numerous pictures of Mainport's "golden girl." Vaulting up from his chair, he lifted a frame off the wall, but he couldn't find it in himself to discard it in one of the empty boxes he'd been filling up with Merrill's personal things. "What the hell am I going to do about you?" he asked the seven-year-old child who sat happily atop a small pony being led by a proud Merrill around the grounds.

Replacing the picture on the wall, he glanced at the clock and realized he'd been brooding for nearly half an hour. There was still a lot of work to be done before he joined Laura and Tom Anderson that afternoon. He hadn't gathered all the figures that would prove to Laura that he knew his job, that he belonged at the Cliffs as much as she, but prove it he would.

5

H e's what?" Tom Anderson exploded, taking Laura's elbow in an unnecessarily firm grasp as they walked into the living room.

"Ryder's staying here," Laura repeated, not displeased that Tom found Ryder's occupancy of her house as unacceptable as she did. "He claims the inn is full and that Gramps invited him to stay here."

"I'm sorry, Laura." Tom's hazel eyes narrowed with self-disgust. "My letter didn't prepare you for this. I thought Bantel would've had the decency to move out until things got settled."

"You knew he was living here?" Laura was shocked. Tom was not only her attorney but one of her oldest and dearest friends, and she couldn't comprehend how he could have withheld such pertinent information.

Avoiding her eyes, Tom placed his briefcase down on

the coffee table and waited for Laura to take her seat on the couch before he sat down beside her and offered an explanation. "I knew, but I certainly didn't expect him to stay on in the house after you arrived."

Shaking his head, he listened to Laura's heated description of her homecoming and her anger with Ryder Bantel for refusing to discuss anything with her that might explain his proprietary attitude toward the Cliffs. "You're my attorney, Tom, and I want you to give me all the facts right now."

She didn't like the look on Tom's face, noting the agitated movement of his hands as he reached for his briefcase and opened the catches. Considering his red hair and the temperament to match, she was astonished that he looked more subdued than angered by her description of the previous day and her feelings about Ryder. As if preparing himself for some ordeal that lay ahead, he took a deep breath, then offered yet another apology. "We've discovered a codicil to your grandfather's will, Laura. Bantel is supposed to be present when I read it to you."

It seemed to Laura as if everyone intended to keep her in the dark as long as possible, and she was growing very tired of it. "I've had a suspicion that something was wrong ever since I received your letter. I don't care if Ryder is here or not, Tom. You tell me what he's got to do with this. Why is that man so concerned with this business?"

Clearing his throat uncomfortably, Tom recognized the obstinate thrust of her chin and knew she was fast losing her temper. "Your grandfather was convinced that Bantel could turn the inn's fortunes around."

Laura frowned, confused. "I thought the Cliffs was

doing as well as it's always done. Gramps never men
tioned that business was down."

Tom was forced by Laura's tight grip on his arm to
elaborate. "The Cliffs has barely broken even over the
past few years. It needed repairs and updating, and
those things really cut into the profit. Laura . . . I
. . . We can't go on with this until Bantel gets here."

As if on cue, the man in question came through the
front door, pausing in the foyer to hang up his rain
dripping slicker and running a hand over his wet hair.
Like Tom, he was carrying a briefcase, but there the
resemblance stopped. Tom looked every inch a lawyer
in his three-piece pin-striped suit, while Ryder still wore
the dark cords and casual sweater he'd had on at
breakfast. He nodded briefly at Laura before offering
his hand to Tom, then lowered himself into a chair
opposite the sofa. Laura couldn't prevent her
exasperated sigh as both men began shuffling in their
briefcases. If their intent was to increase her anxiety by behaving as if they were preparing cases in a
trial, they couldn't have been more successful. "Can't
we get on with this?"

"Of course, Laura." Tom lifted the top paper from his
briefcase, then reached for her hand, holding it tightly.
Looking across at Ryder, Laura felt a bit smug when she
caught his disapproving glance on their clasped hands.
He now knew that she had Tom's full support and that
he'd have to contend with the both of them.

An hour later, Laura had to acknowledge that neither
she nor Tom could do anything to change what Ryder
had arranged with her grandfather. Merrill Davis had
sold fifty-one percent of the property to Ryder Bantel
and had used the money from the sale to pay off his

outstanding debts. With the exception of the Morrisons' cottage, Ryder owned controlling interest in the entire Davis property.

Laura sat like a statue and listened as Ryder offered to buy out her forty-nine percent, despising the businesslike clip in his voice that signified total control as he urged Tom to convince her to accept fair market value for her share of the property. Neither man in the room—nor even her grandfather—had considered that she would have wanted to live at the Cliffs and carry on the family tradition. Because she was a woman, attractive and single, they had assumed she would yearn for a different life style, but worse, Laura thought, they had judged her incapable of running the restaurant and inn by herself.

Feeling betrayed, Laura broke into the conversation going on between Tom and Ryder. "You're to be commended, Mr. Bantel, for not laughing while I made a complete fool of myself yesterday." The bitter twist to her lips was accompanied by angry tears shimmering in her large eyes.

She had the satisfaction of seeing a slight tinge of pink come up on Ryder's jaw before he regained the smooth control he had maintained since their meeting began. "You weren't in full possession of the facts." Ryder implied that he was willing to forget the overconfident statements she had made about taking over the inn and dismissing him. She wasn't.

"But you were," she said sarcastically, deliberately snubbing him by turning her attention to Tom. "Why?" she asked shortly, not sure Tom didn't deserve her censure as much as Ryder. "Why didn't you or my grandfather inform me of this? The inn was never intended to make anyone rich, but we've always been well provided for. What happened?''

Tom slid a comforting arm around her quivering shoulders, and she had to bite her tongue to keep herself from ordering him to remove it. She wanted an explanation, not comfort. She was not a small child who couldn't understand what was going on.

"Laura, you know that Merrill never liked worrying you about anything," Tom said, trying to placate her. "He didn't want to saddle you with a business that was in a decline. In his own way, he was trying to make things easy on you. He knew Mr. Bantel would offer to buy you out, and if you don't want to sell, you'll still be provided with a steady income from your share."

The two men exchanged glances, and Tom added hurriedly, "But as your lawyer, it's my opinion you'd be better off taking Mr. Bantel's offer. It's more than fair."

Moving her penetrating gray eyes from one man to the other, she declared, "I'm not ready to make that kind of decision just yet." Then, centering the force of her gaze solely on Ryder, she continued sardonically, "However, I do owe you an apology, Mr. Bantel. Since this house is more yours than mine, I had no right to ask you to leave." Standing up, she forced herself to maintain a calm she was far from feeling. "I'll move in with the Morrisons until I've reached a decision."

"Now, Laura . . ." Tom stood up at her side. "I know you're upset, but—"

"The apology is mine." Ryder sprang up from his chair, preventing her from making a dramatic exit by blocking her way. "I'll move over to the inn. You might not credit me with any sensitivity, Laura"—he stressed his persistent refusal to revert to a last-name basis—

"but this has always been your home, and it will be until you decide differently."

Big of you, Laura silently berated him, unable to let him get away with the supposedly gallant gesture when she knew there wasn't a courteous bone in his body. "But the inn is full. There's no place for you to—"

"It's full until the end of the season." Ryder interrupted. "I can sleep on a cot in the office until then, and we won't need to inconvenience the Morrisons. Their place is too small for guests, and besides, it wouldn't be fair to ask them to change their normal routine because of something this simple to work out."

The man was an underhanded swine for making it sound as if her proposal took only herself into consideration while he magnanimously catered to everyone's needs but his own. Recognizing the mocking sparkle in Ryder's blue eyes, she was very aware that he was trying to manipulate her, but she was desperate for some time alone to lick her wounds and thought that it was fitting for him to be the one to suffer for it. Sending that message with her eyes, she said something entirely different. "I'm grateful for your perception, Ryder. Sophie's place is too small for guests, so if you really wouldn't mind sleeping at the inn for one night, I'd greatly appreciate the sacrifice."

His expression showed that he'd underestimated her and was irritated by having the tables neatly turned on him. She didn't see the fleeting glint of admiration in his eyes as she cemented her position by brushing away a stray tear that had escaped through her lids and was silently rolling down one pale cheek.

"Take all the time you need, Laura." Ryder's eyes followed the movement of her hand as if he couldn't make up his mind whether or not her tears were genuine. "But before we break up this meeting, I have thought of another alternative you might like to consider."

Curious despite her mistrust of him, Laura shrugged her shoulders and sat down on the arm of the sofa, waving her hand at Tom to retake his seat. As soon as Tom was comfortable, she slid her arm along the back of the sofa, resting her fingers on Tom's shoulders as she nodded for Ryder to go on.

"I could buy out your portion of the inn, and you could buy my portion of the house. You'd end up with a sizable profit, and you wouldn't have the worry of being involved in running the inn." Ryder's tone indicated he thought it an equitable offer, but Laura thought otherwise.

"I'm sure that would suit your purposes very well, but money's not the issue here. I'm not the type to sit around and collect interest on my investments. I was looking forward to working at the inn. I want to be involved."

"I could give you a job," Ryder stated obligingly, astonished by the pugnacious expression still apparent on her face. "Damn it, Laura"—the southern accent was again in evidence—"I'm willing to give you the house plus a sizable chunk of money. I want to get on with my plans, and I'm not interested in who occupies the house. If you want it, it's yours, and we'll both get what we want. You can work at the inn or go back to teaching. What more could you want?"

"For an astute businessman, that's an incredibly one-sided offer," Laura shot back, preventing Tom from entering the conversation by squeezing his shoulder. "But since we're discussing what we want, let me present an additional alternative apparently neither one of you have considered."

Gracefully, she slid off the arm of the sofa and walked to the fireplace, feeling both men's eyes burning into her back. Turning around, she stood drumming her finger tips on the smooth mantel, staring up at the oil painting of the old mansion that had been done by her great-great-grandmother almost five generations ago. Whatever Ryder thought, she was not going to be the one to lose out on the legacy handed down by those hard-working people. Planting her feet firmly in the soft carpet, she spoke in a calm, clear voice. "I would've liked to have thought about this for a while longer, but looking around this room, I realize I've already made up my mind. I'm not selling my interest in the inn or this house or the land surrounding them. I may not own all of it, but I will retain what I have."

"Laura." Tom's voice was soothing, as if he thought her too overwrought to reason wisely. "Bantel's offer is extremely generous. With the money you make from the sale, you could live comfortably for the rest of your life. I know I could invest your funds in a way that would ensure you a substantial income."

"No," Laura said through gritted teeth. Tom's continued insistence that she should sell was beginning to grate on her nerves. "I'm a Davis—the last Davis. I belong right here."

Backing down from the defiant look on her face, Tom accepted her decision, but they both knew he planned to bring it up again after she'd had a few days to cool down. What Tom didn't know was that there was nothing he could say to change her mind, for she wasn't reacting from shock but was motivated by the inner conviction that her future happiness depended on her retaining at least some ownership of the Cliffs. Even though Ryder owned a larger share of the property, he wasn't enriched by its history, as she was, nor did he need it to attain fulfillment. To him, the inn was a failing enterprise he was determined to make a success; to her, the inn represented security, family, and peace. She'd make sure he didn't take those things away from her. One day, she was certain, Ryder would move on to other, more interesting places, but she was home for good.

"I do think Ryder's on the right track here," Tom said, stacking his papers back inside his case. "He's got some good ideas for changing this place, Laura. I'm not sure you'll enjoy staying when there will be nothing you can do to prevent him from continuing on with his plans."

"That remains to be seen," Laura gritted stubbornly, a bit shaken that a man she had always considered a loyal friend appeared to be swaying toward the opposition. Swinging around to Ryder, she exploded in a vitriolic attack. She was particularly incensed because Tom had pointed out her helpless position.

"Just what kind of grandiose ideas does the hot shot from the big city have for this humble establishment? I'm warning you, Ryder. I'll block you every step of the way if you intend to turn the Cliffs into some garish tourist trap. You may have the legal control to do what you want, but I know this area, and I can get enough support from the county commissioner to stop you dead in your tracks. We've done fine without your expert help for years and will continue doing fine long after you've gone."

Breathless after her tirade, Laura still had enough

control left to be acutely aware of what she'd done. If she thought she'd seen Ryder angry before, it was nothing compared to now. Like a sleeping tiger being provoked awake by a pesky fly, his blue eyes blazed explosively. A muscle clenched along his jaw, and his wide mouth was set in a determinedly thin line.

"I'm going to assume you're making idle threats," he stated quietly and deliberately, dismissing her words as easily as the tiger would have waved off the fly. "I know you've just had a shock, so I'm going to leave you two alone to discuss what's happened. Before I leave, however, I'll give you some free advice. I won't tolerate interference in my business decisions, and you'll be making a large mistake if you attempt to get in my way."

He spoke in a low, growling voice that had the same ominous effect of distant thunder before an approaching storm. "I'm not here to satisfy some whim, and you'll quickly discover how far I'm willing to go if you make things difficult."

Shielding herself behind a cloak of false bravado, Laura watched him walk to the door but couldn't let him have the last word. "I think I've got a good idea how far you'll go, Ryder. I learned your tactics last night, and they won't have any more effect on me now than they did then. You may not like it any more than I, but you won't be able to do one thing to stop me if I choose to make things as difficult as I can."

"Won't I, Laura?" He drawled dangerously, a now-familiar inflection in his parting shot. "Don't take on more than you can handle."

Shaking with impotent rage, Laura felt ready to explode until Tom came to her side and pulled her against his chest, offering her the comfort of his familiar arms. "He hasn't touched you, Laura? He hasn't hurt you?"

"Of course not," Laura negated quickly, ashamed to admit that Ryder had kissed her and that she'd enjoyed it. Self-disgust poisoned her tone as she cried, "He just showed me what a dishonest, back-stabbing, co—"

"Simmer down, Laura," Tom advised her, recognizing the posture that had always betrayed an upcoming tempest. "This whole thing got out of hand. I know you may hate me for saying this, but Bantel is a reasonable man. It's not his fault that Merrill sold out to him. He's holding all the cards, and you'll only hurt yourself if you go on like this."

Unsure where the lawyer stood, Laura didn't feel it was wise to reveal the full extent of her feelings toward Ryder, but she did intend to make sure Tom wouldn't continue trying to convince her to sell. "I was angry, and I suppose I got carried away. I just can't bear the thought of a man like him, someone who only cares about turning a profit, having control of this place. I know it's a big white elephant to some, but it's one of the last old mansions along the shore, and it should be preserved, not changed. If that supercilious bas—"

"Okay, now," Tom warned her, shaking a finger under her chin as he stepped back to release her. "You're gearing up for another round, but I'm in your corner. I will say that if you're going to do business with Bantel, you'll have to keep things in perspective and stay cool. He's years ahead of you in this business, and he won't be moved by emotional onslaughts."

Laura agreed. "It was foolish to lose control like that. I wasn't thinking."

Tom placed his hands on her shoulders and looked deeply into her eyes. "Then, as your lawyer, I have to

71

ask if you were thinking straight when you turned down his offer? It's a lot of money, Laura."

"The money's just not important to me, Tom," Laura admitted. "It never was."

"Obviously," Tom said dryly, "but it's not too late to change your mind." His grin stretched wider when he saw the warning flash of amber in her eyes. "But I'll always be there for you, Laura, whatever you decide."

As if nothing had changed between them since their high school days, Laura was comforted by Tom's affectionate words. "I know that, Tom." She smiled, glad she could still count on him. "I keep forgetting that you're obligated to dispense sound advice."

They linked arms as they walked out of the living room into the foyer, pausing at the bottom of the stairs as Laura teased, "I always think of you as my knight in shining armor, counselor. It was disconcerting to hear you advising me to sell when I thought you'd come to save a damsel in distress."

"Would it help if I asked you out to dinner later in the week and promised not to talk business? I suppose I could pick you up on a white horse. I think Lars Nelson still boards a few on his place."

Relaxing beneath the companionable banter they'd always enjoyed together, Laura accepted his invitation, astonished when he placed his briefcase down on the floor and drew her into his arms. "Welcome home, Laura," he murmured before kissing her.

Although the kiss was of short duration, it wasn't at all brotherly, and Laura was too surprised to say anything when he abruptly released her, picked up his case, and strode to the door. "I've missed you, Laura. I'll call you tonight." He grinned and was gone.

"Very touching." Ryder was standing at the top of

the stairs, and it was obvious he'd been there for quite some time. His gaze was centered on her parted lips as he descended the stairs. "Is he part of the reason you came back to stay?"

Laura saw no reason to explain her relationship with Tom to him and said nothing as she started up the stairs. Intending to slip past him as if he weren't there, she was startled when he grabbed hold of her arm.

"What would he say if I told him I've held your half-naked body in my arms?"

She was warned by the prolonged stress he gave each syllable and was more and more curious about his background, but it definitely wasn't a wise time to ask. It was time to prove he couldn't get to her with that kind of threat. "Tom wouldn't believe you," she said simply, pulling her arm away from him. "We have a civilized relationship built on mutual respect."

His drawled promise followed her the rest of the way up the stairs. "Push me too far, Laura, and you'll find out you're no more civilized than I. In fact, I tapped into a beautifully untamed part of you last night, and that intrigues me. I'd really enjoy bringing that passion out in you again, and we both know I could do it."

She did know, but he wasn't ever going to hear her admit it. "Don't bother," she called when there was a safe distance between them. "Last night, I was emotionally drained. If I responded to you, I must have been temporarily insane. You're definitely not my type and never will be."

She heard the door slam, and it was the perfect punctuation for the end of her contemptuous statement. She'd finally scored a point in one of their verbal skirmishes, and she hugged that small pleasure to herself as she gained her bedroom and went inside.

6

~~~~~~~~~~

Laura sat at the kitchen table, lingering over her second cup of coffee as she stared out at the lake through the bay window. The choppy gray waves were shrouded by rolling mists that rose in miniature columns above the waves. The lake was still showing the effects of the previous day's torrential rain, but by noon the bright sun would burn off the cool fog, and the lake's surface would become placid, almost as if soothed by the warm rays. Unfortunately, Laura knew a sunny day would not help her recover from the emotional storm she'd weathered.

She'd gone to dinner the night before at the Morrisons' cabin, expecting Sophie and Will to sympathize with her; she instead, found that the opposite was true. Not only did the elderly couple approve of Ryder's presence at the inn, but also they felt that Laura would be wise to accept his offer to buy out her share. Laura couldn't help but notice that her two friends had declined in health over the years and felt a surge of guilt for ever having considered moving in with them. They told her that they greatly appreciated Ryder's concern for their future and informed her that he'd made sure there would always be a home for them at the Cliffs even if Laura sold out. They felt their future was secure in Ryder's capable hands, but Laura didn't share their trust in him. Even though she understood the Morrisons' viewpoint, she still felt as if she'd been deserted by everyone.

The sound of the front door opening and closing, then heavy footsteps ascending the stairs, brought her out of her depressing contemplations. No one but Ryder would have the nerve to let himself into the house unannounced. That firm step was made by a man who knew where he was going and didn't consider that anyone might stand in his way.

"Damn the man!" she cursed, slamming her cup down on its saucer. She was further incensed when the warm coffee stained the crisp white cloth that covered the table and sloshed onto her slacks. Grabbing a napkin, she dabbed angrily at the spots on her pressed khaki slacks and the tablecloth, then scraped her chair back from the table.

She marched out of the kitchen and up the stairs, determined to give Ryder Bantel a piece of her mind, but found herself choking on the angry words when she encountered Ryder in the hall. He had just stepped out of his bedroom, wearing nothing but a terry sarong that barely covered his loins. She not only forgot her speech but also how to breathe as her large gray eyes became glued to the magnificent panorama of bronze flesh displayed so enticingly in front of her. Her heart began beating at what she felt sure was twice the speed of sound. Never had she experienced such a strong sexual response to a man, and she didn't like it. Why did it have to be a man like him who could turn her bones to water just by looking at him?

"Good morning, Laura," Ryder greeted. "Was there something you wanted?" The solicitous inquiry was accompanied by a lazy grin that showed her he was well aware of her reaction to him.

"What do you think you're doing?" Laura managed in the vain hope he'd attribute her breathlessness to her rapid climb up the stairs.

"What does it look like?" His blue eyes gleamed with mischief as he placed a hand on his hip and took a step toward her. "I'm on my way to take a shower. You're welcome to join me. I certainly enjoyed the last time we shared the bathroom."

Refusing to be baited by his suggestive taunt, Laura swiftly rekindled her anger. "I thought even a man like you might give me some kind of warning before coming back."

The mischievous glint died in his eyes, and his voice dropped to a rasping whisper. "A man like me?"

She was too carried away with temper to be aware that she had suddenly stepped onto very dangerous ground. "Yes, a man who was obviously never taught common courtesy. You could've given me some notice instead of barging in like this."

"I haven't come calling, ma'am," Ryder drawled in that superficially polite way of his that caused the hair to rise on the back of her neck. "I live here and can come and go as I please."

"I live here, too," Laura retorted, lifting her chin defiantly. "But I was raised to respect other people's privacy. We need to set down some ground rules right now."

Prepared for another melodious comment that would prove how angry she'd made him, she was astonished by his clipped, even tone. "I agree. Since we're going to be living together, we should discuss the arrangements." He rubbed his arms, which were covered with goose flesh. "May I please have your permission to take a shower first, Miss Davis?"

"Of course," Laura snapped defensively, unable to keep her eyes from the dark hairs rising on his arms and chest. To keep him from noticing her increasing interest, she turned on her heel and marched to the stairs. "I'll wait for you in the kitchen."

On the second step down, she flung over her shoulder, "And I'd rather you didn't call our arrangement living together."

An amused chuckle followed her retreat, "Yes, ma'am," he shouted back before closing the bathroom door behind him.

Ryder joined her in the kitchen twenty minutes later. He had changed into a pair of khaki slacks and a pale yellow short-sleeved shirt, which was almost the same outfit Laura had chosen for herself. She wondered if he'd dressed like that deliberately but wasn't about to start another argument with him by asking.

"Any coffee left?" he inquired, waiting for her affirmative nod before walking to the stove and pouring himself a cup.

She didn't say anything as he came to the table and casually lowered his tall frame onto the chair opposite hers. Leaning back, he took a sip of his coffee, smiled at the taste, then gave her his full attention, his blue eyes expectant.

Laura cleared her throat, then began speaking in a level tone. "I'm going to live here, Ryder, and work at the inn. There's nothing you can say to get me to change my mind, so don't even bother. What we need to do now is decide how we're going to work this out."

"I'm sure you have some plan in mind." Ryder's expression didn't change.

"Yes, I do." Laura had used the entire time he was in the shower to devise an equitable plan even though she angrily resented the unexpected need for one. She judged him to be the kind of man who'd admire straightforwardness, so she got right to the point. "I want to be directly involved in all decisions made about the inn. You may have the controlling interest, but I own a major portion of the business and want to be treated as a partner. As far as sharing this house goes, it won't work. I suggest one of us take rooms at the inn."

Ignoring her statement about the business, he addressed himself to their living arrangements. "I've already told you that the inn is full to capacity until the end of the season. The other hotels in the area are also booked solid. Neither one of us may like it, but the only accommodations available are in this house. I'm not having a problem with that. What's yours?"

Usually capable of responding to logic with logic, Laura floundered. He knew exactly what kind of a problem she had but was counting on her not being able to verbalize it. If she told him she was afraid of what people might say, he'd laugh at her archaic attitude. If she told him she was afraid she'd eventually end up in his bed, he'd have proof out of her own lips what kind of effect he was having on her, and she didn't want to give him any additional leverage. He had more than enough as it was. "Would it do any good if I told you?"

"Probably not," Ryder admitted, challenging her with his eyes.

"So it's settled, then, no matter what I think, isn't it?" Laura snapped angrily. "Another example to prove to me that whenever we don't agree, you'll win."

"Not at all." Ryder laughed, as if he thought she were blowing the whole thing out of proportion. "Do you have any logical reasons for us not sharing this house?"

"Not that you'd consider logical." Laura dropped her eyes, her hostility toward him increasing with each passing second. This was one situation she'd never imagined happening to her, and the twenty minutes of preparation she'd had to confront him hadn't been enough. From then on, she planned to think before she spoke and not let him unsettle her to the point where he could twist everything she said to his own advantage.

"Since that's resolved, let's discuss the practical aspects. How do you want it to work? Shall we divide all the chores fifty-fifty, or shall each of us be responsible for themselves?"

Resigned to the situation until she could come up with a reasonable argument to convince him otherwise, Laura declared firmly, "I'll look after myself, and you can do the same."

"Agreed." Ryder came back quickly. "See how simple this is turning out to be? Now let's get on to business. The restaurant is going to be understaffed until the end of the season. You can start by helping out in the kitchen."

"The kitchen!" Laura shouted, the amber flecks in her eyes igniting for battle.

"It's only two weeks until the season is over, and that's a job that needs doing." Ryder's pitch slipped a full octave lower. "I don't have time right now to bring you up-to-date on the financial end of things. In the meantime, I thought you could help me out at the restaurant. Unless a Davis is only capable of being an attractive ornament behind the reservations desk."

"You'd be surprised what a Davis is capable of." Laura's expression was murderous. "I've worked at every position there is at the inn, including standing over that hot grill flipping hamburgers."

"I'm not sure if I believe that, but this would be a great time to prove me wrong. I'm not much use over there. I could wait on tables, but they've got that under control."

Laura had never dealt with a more exasperating man in her life. "And what will the exalted manager of the Cliffs be doing while I'm washing dishes and frying hamburgers?"

"Since you're so experienced, you know how much paper work is involved in closing the inn." Ryder got up from his chair and walked toward the back door. "It's the final two weeks of the season, so you can bet I'll be busy."

She was certain he was suppressing a grin as he opened the door and called back over his shoulder, "You'd better hurry if you want to get caught up with the dishes before the lunch crowd arrives. Oh, and tomorrow, you'll have to report by six. Should I tell the cook to expect you?"

He was just daring her to say no, but she was determined to show him she was willing to do any job necessary for the good of the inn. "With bells on," she sallied sarcastically.

"Then we should get along just fine." Ryder grinned and sauntered out the door.

By late afternoon, she was still venting her anger with

him on the dirty dishes in the inn's kitchen. She loaded the industrial dishwasher to capacity again and again, scrubbed down the stainless-steel counters, swept the floors, and found she still had enough head of steam to accept Tom's invitation to dinner.

She surprised herself by having a good time and was grateful to Tom for taking her mind off her troubles. It was almost like old times except that when Tom brought her home in the wee hours and kissed her good night, she couldn't respond. He'd accepted the excuse that she was tired, but she knew it wasn't that. As soon as she noticed that the back-porch light had been turned on for her, she got an uncomfortable mental image of Ryder waiting up for her, which was totally ridiculous and shouldn't have bothered her. Nevertheless, the thought unnerved her so much she couldn't enjoy Tom's embrace.

She felt oddly let down, upon entering the house, to find that Ryder had already gone to bed, obviously not the least interested in her whereabouts. The next morning, she suffered for having stayed out so late the night before but managed to keep her eyes open until she'd finished her work in the kitchen. She'd only seen Ryder once, when he'd stuck his head around the kitchen door to inquire if she'd seen Will. She'd expected him to make some nasty comment about the dark circles under her eyes, but he'd barely waited for her negative nod before he'd ducked back out the door in search of Will. She managed to avoid running into him the rest of the day, and before he got in for the night, she'd eaten a light supper and had dropped into bed, totally exhausted.

The final two weeks of the season progressed, with Laura reporting each morning to the kitchen, slaving over the hot grill, then spending hours up to her elbows in water as she scrubbed down the counters and grill. She took all of her meals at the inn with her friends from the kitchen, telling herself it wasn't because she didn't want to eat with Ryder at the house but because it saved time. She took a two-hour break during the afternoons, enjoying the camaraderie of the staff, some of whom she'd known for years, occasionally taking a refreshing dip in the lake, then returning to the kitchen until after the dinner hour. She worked like a demon until the last pot was scrubbed and put away, then would drag herself back to the house to take a bath and fall into bed. She never complained and even managed to go out with Tom a few more times, but because she had to be up so early in the mornings, they never stayed out as late as they had that first night.

As the days passed, her fears about sharing a house with Ryder completely dissipated. She never saw him, and oddly enough, that was beginning to bother her a great deal. In the beginning, he'd behaved as if he thought her a desirable woman, but since she'd informed him of her position, he'd barely spoken to her, let alone attempted to make love to her again.

She knew he came back to the house to sleep every night, but she rarely heard him come in, and he was gone before she let herself out in the morning. She gave him credit for having fastidious personal habits, for she never saw any evidence of his having used the bathroom, the kitchen, or any other room in the house. She began hoping he'd leave a mess somewhere so she wouldn't feel so guilty whenever she left something out of place. Sometimes, being tired, she was tempted not to pick up her clothes at night or wash the dishes after a late-night snack, but since Ryder was always meticulous, she forced herself to behave the same way. She'd taken to peeking into his bedroom on the way out of the house to see if he always made his bed. He always did! Lately, she'd caught herself talking to him even though he was never there to hear her half-deprecating, half-pleading remarks. "Hospital corners yet! Can't you at least drop some toothpaste on the sink once in a while? I want a coffee ring on the table, Ryder. Just one." Then imagining how he'd react if he heard her, she commanded herself not to think about him, but her irate ramblings grew more and more frequent as the season came to an end.

On the last Saturday of the month, the final patron checked out, and Laura was free to spend the evening in any way she chose. Turning down the invitation issued by the college-aged staff to join them for a boat party to celebrate the closing of the inn, she decided on a leisurely soak in the tub instead and a long-promised interlude with a current best-seller. Dressed in her most comfortable bathrobe, she had just adjusted the pillows on her bed into position when the phone rang. Thinking it was Tom, she thought up an excuse for turning him down, too, so she was taken off guard when she picked up the phone and heard Ryder's clipped voice.

"Calling it a night?" Ryder asked without preamble.

"What?" Laura wasn't sure what prompted his question and wanted more information before admitting anything. If he was calling to complain that she had stopped work too early, he was going to get an earful, but she'd learned enough about him not to jump to any hasty conclusions.

"I saw your bedroom light," Ryder informed smoothly. "I wanted to know if you're so tired you're going to bed or if you're getting ready to go out for the evening, since you didn't join the others on the boat."

"Why do you want to know?" Laura hedged, still not sure where the conversation was heading.

There was a significant pause before he said anything, and when he did, he was using that slight southern accent of his. If she'd gotten one opportunity, she'd have asked him where he acquired it, but they hadn't talked for days, and once again she decided it wasn't the appropriate time. She knew that the accent only occurred when he was very angry, but she was unaware of anything that could have happened to prompt it. "Tom called here asking for you. I assume he reached you?"

"Not yet."

"I told him I was still working and assumed you were, too. But you're not, are you?"

So that's it. Laura was beginning to understand why Ryder was angry. He thought she was going out to have some fun while he was still wrapping things up over at the inn. Well, he hadn't asked for her assistance, and she wasn't about to offer any. If he wanted to work all night, that was his business, but he needn't expect her to do the same.

When she didn't immediately answer his question, he demanded, "Are you going out with Tom?"

"Is that any of your business?" she inquired in a saccharine voice that only served to antagonize him further.

"It is if you're planning to go out tonight," he announced, the fluid syllables falling from his tongue like honey. "The inn may be closed, but that doesn't mean the work is done."

Since his drawl was more pronounced than she'd ever heard it, Laura gave in even though she would have liked to let him dig his hole deeper before she admitted she wasn't going anywhere. "I don't have plans with Tom, and I don't know what work you're talking about. If you wanted me to help you with something, you only had to ask."

Although there was no softening in tone, there was also no accent as Ryder said, "I've finished up over here, but I'd like to go over some figures with you tonight. I thought you'd probably want to know about some changes I'm planning, but if you're too tired . . ." His voice trailed off.

"I see." Laura couldn't help it; she rose to the bait exactly as she was certain he wanted. "And just when do these changes go into effect?"

"Starting next week."

"Next week!" Laura repeated, her syrupy tone quickly replaced by tartness. She could feel the blood coming to a simmering boil in her veins. "Delayed until the last minute, didn't you? Is that because you're positive I'm going to agree with these changes? Or could it be you didn't dare give me more time to come up with some means of stopping you if I don't like what you're going to tell me? For some reason, I didn't expect you to take the coward's way out." Now that she was on a roll, she couldn't seem to stop. "Of course, I should have learned from my past experience. You didn't have the guts to tell me who you were the night we met or set me straight when I told you my plans to fire you."

"Laura, I—"

"No explanations are necessary, Ryder," Laura interjected angrily. "I don't have to like it, do I? That's what this whole thing is all about."

"You haven't liked what I've told you since the first time we met." Ryder sounded tired, almost defeated, and it was completely out of character. "I am human, you know, and it's natural for us lesser mortals to avoid trouble. You may think you operate on a loftier plane than I, but I haven't noticed you frantically trying to get in touch with me, so it cuts both ways, doesn't it?"

Astonished by his defensiveness, she didn't know what to say. It was the first time he'd indicated he was troubled by her behavior, but she couldn't tell if he was concerned about possible interference in his future plans for the inn or if he was uneasy about his reactions to her as a woman. Oddly enough, she found she wanted confirmation of the last much more than the first. "What trouble are you trying to avoid?" she probed softly.

"Offending you more than I already have, damn it." Ryder sounded as if he'd come to the end of his patience. "Your message has come across loud and clear, lady, but I've had it."

"I don't have any idea what you're talking about." Laura's confusion was apparent in her voice. "I've given you nothing to complain about."

"Good Lord, woman." Ryder began relaying his frustrations. "You could have had the decency to leave some dirty laundry in the hamper or forget to scrub out the tub once in a while. Not only have you done a fine job of convincing me you're as capable as I am; you've also effectively proved that as far as you're concerned, I don't exist. I'm too damned tired to keep this up, Laura. When I get home tonight, I'm throwing all my clothes on the floor and leaving wet towels in the bathroom."

Thinking about the innumerable times she'd been exasperated by the same feelings, Laura couldn't help it; she burst out laughing. "What a relief! I thought I was trapped in a house with Felix Unger. If I'd found the newspaper neatly refolded and placed on the coffee table one more time, I'd have set it on fire and placed it under one of those damned hospital corners you make on your bed."

His booming laughter erupted over the receiver. Laura loved the sound of it and found herself wishing he were in the room with her so she could see his face. "Let's make a deal," he said, chuckling. "You stop shining the toaster, and I'll stop scouring the coffeepot. Agreed?"

"Agreed." Laura leaned back on the pillows.

"Wish I'd have known you'd been nosing around in my bedroom. That would have given me some hope that you didn't find me totally repulsive."

"I was looking for dust balls, Ryder, not succumbing to burning feminine curiosity about your sleeping habits."

"Not nice"—Ryder chuckled—"and I'm not far off base when I imagine you as a lioness who'd love making me her next kill."

Instead of being insulted, Laura liked that image, and it was exciting to discover he'd been thinking about her. Thoughts about him certainly occupied a great deal of her time. Since he was being so forthcoming, she returned the favor. "I often think of you as a rebel raider who's dared to cross this far into enemy territory." As soon as she said it, she wanted to follow through and ask him about his accent, but he didn't give her the chance.

"Perhaps we'd better get back to business."

She noticed that his southern drawl was missing and had the strangest sensation that it was by deliberate effort. Was he ashamed of his accent? Even though he usually resorted to it when he was angry, she found it very attractive. Still, their relationship was very shaky, and she didn't want to risk losing the ground they'd gained. "Were you serious about going over those figures with me tonight?"

"Sorry." His apology was genuine. "I know I've left this to the last minute, and you might be right about my motives, but if you want to have your say, it'll have to be tonight."

"All right." Laura sighed. "Give me a few minutes to get dressed and I'll come over."

It only took him a second to consider and discard that offer. "I'll come there. That way, if you fall asleep during one of my lengthier dissertations, I'll only have to carry you up the stairs. I'll be right there."

Unaware that she hadn't said good-by, Laura swallowed hard and put the receiver back on its hook. She scrambled off the bed and raced to the closet. She removed her favorite sun dress from a hanger and held it up in front of her. The soft peach material would offset her golden complexion and highlight her hair. She stepped into the dress and fastened the tiny pearl buttons that reached from the low neckline to the scalloped hem. Going to the mirror, she hurriedly began reapplying her makeup. Her hair was an impossible tangle of damp blond curls, but she brushed it out as best she could and was almost presentable by the time she heard Ryder open the front door downstairs.

"I'll be right down," she shouted, then slipped her feet into a pair of sandals and took a last glance in the mirror. There was an excited sparkle in her gray eyes, and a becoming flush had come up on her cheeks that made the rose tone she'd applied unnecessary. Grabbing a Kleenex, she scrubbed off the rouge and scolded the woman in the mirror. "This isn't a date, lady. You're meeting a man who wants you to keep your nose out of his business. Remember that." But she forgot the instant she walked out of her room and regretted her lapse long before their meeting was over.

7

Good evening, Laura," Ryder greeted from the bottom of the stairs. A congenial smile spread across his wide sensual mouth as his eyes traveled from her shining head, down her face, then to her lightly tanned shoulders, exposed by the piqué sun dress. "You look lovely tonight." His voice was deep and rich, his eyes lingering on her fitted bodice as she descended the stairs.

"Thank you." Laura smiled at him from the bottom step, then preceded him into the living room. About to tell him to make himself at home, she realized he might take it wrong, and she didn't want to say anything that would disrupt the tentative peace they'd established over the phone.

From the beginning, she'd found him a difficult man to understand. The things that provoked him always came as a surprise to her, for he shrugged off more complex issues with ease. Perhaps he was the kind of person who easily grasped overall issues but became frustrated with small details. Remembering those times she'd set off his anger—when she referred to his rise from a waiter to the owner of his own business or made caustic remarks about his upbringing and manner—she decided that there was something in his past he'd not yet been able to put behind him. Perhaps it was a woman. She hoped not, for the thought of Ryder's being involved with another woman filled her with an unreasonable jealousy.

Walking across the room, she switched on a lamp, determined to keep everything on a friendly basis as she turned back to him. He was bending down to place a folder and several long rolls of paper on the coffee table, and she became fascinated by the ripple of powerful muscles beneath the smooth fabric of his light blue shirt. His broad back narrowed to the waistband of his dark slacks, which stretched enticingly across his hips. He had the physique of a college athlete, and she wondered how he managed to retain the rock-hard muscles that flexed with every move he made. While she stood admiring him, he took a seat on the sofa. His knowing smile jolted her thoughts back to the business at hand.

"I think I'll make some coffee. Would you like some?" she asked, breaking the unsettling eye contact by taking a step toward the kitchen.

"I'd rather have a drink if you don't mind," Ryder answered, and Laura offered to bring him some ice from the kitchen after she'd made her coffee.

A few minutes later, she returned, carrying a small bucket of ice in one hand and her coffee cup in the other. In three strides, he was by her side, gallantly relieving her of the bucket. She inwardly trembled when his fingers lingered on hers, his blue eyes penetrating hers for what seemed like an eternity before he turned away and walked to the bar. Nervously, she hurried to the sofa and sat down. She took a sip of coffee, then, without looking at him, asked, "So what's on your mind, Ryder?"

"Hopefully, the same thing that's on yours," Ryder drawled suggestively from behind her before he took his seat on the other end of the sofa. He stretched one arm along the back, saluted her with his glass, then raised it to his lips and took a long swallow. "But I have my doubts."

"I'm curious about the figures you wanted to show me." Laura chose to ignore his innuendo. "And even more curious about the changes you mentioned."

Taking his cue that she wanted to get right down to business, Ryder gave a half-rueful shrug and turned his attention to the papers before him. "Before we get into the changes I propose, I'd like to go over the receipts and expenses accrued this season and compare them with last year's."

He handed her a thick ledger. She opened it and studied the figures, quickly surveying the columns until she reached the profit-loss tabulations. The inn had shown a profit, albeit a small one, but it was enough to provide them with an adequate living.

"It looks like the inn is doing as well as always." Her tone conveyed her confusion. "I don't understand what you're trying to prove by showing me these."

"We only earned a profit because I used my own funds to bail the inn out of debt," he explained curtly. "I've made the immediate repairs, but what happens the next time? There isn't enough profit left over to cover additional expenditures and still leave us a small income. It's been like that for years, and that's not good enough for me anymore."

Laura didn't appreciate the slight note of condescension in his tone. "I don't need a lot of money, Ryder. If you think this is a get-rich-quick proposition, you're mistaken. This is a family resort, and that's what it will stay."

"Look at last year's figures, Laura," Ryder said tersely. "A thriving concern must show an increase in profit every year to remain in business. What's the sense of owning a business if it doesn't make money?"

She no longer had any doubts about his opinion of her business acumen, and the promise she'd made herself to keep in control of her temper went up in smoke. "Obviously, your idea of success and mine are two different things," she exclaimed furiously. "If you want to be a millionaire, why don't you buy a hotel in Atlantic City?"

"Look," Ryder drawled slowly and dangerously, "I'm trying to be patient with you, Laura. Are you so naive you can't see the handwriting on the wall? Times are changing, and if the Cliffs don't change with them, there won't be any profits, large or small. The changes I have in mind will draw a fair share of the tourist trade. Use your head, woman."

Golden fire shot from her eyes. "It's done all right so far and without any hot shot from the East butting in. This place was founded on respected tradition. Maybe that doesn't mean anything to you, but it means a lot to me. My ancestors would roll over in their graves if you turn this place into some garish tourist trap! Money isn't the issue here, Ryder. It's tradition and class!"

"I'm well aware of the kind of tradition represented

here." Ryder glared, shifting his body on the couch until she was as threatened by his proximity as from the indigo daggers slicing from his eyes. "And you're a perfect example of it!"

"What's that supposed to mean?"

"You're the golden girl, aren't you?" His expression was contemptuous. "On the surface, you've got everything, but like that beautiful house over there, you've a potential that's never been tapped. Keep this up, Laura, and I might set a new tradition by showing you what kind of passion you've been hiding beneath that untouchable exterior."

Not only had their truce been broken, but they'd escalated into a full-scale battle. Knowing it might have been wiser to retreat while she still had the chance, Laura couldn't prevent herself from picking up his verbal gauntlet. "You won't show me anything, Ryder Bantel! My grandfather didn't sell you part ownership in me."

"No, he didn't. You weren't any part of the deal." His slow delivery frightened her. "But maybe when he made me manager, he had you in mind. Someone should have forced you back in line years ago. You're not going to find me as easy to handle as your grandfather."

"Well, that's fine, because I don't want anything more to do with you!"

"Like hell," Ryder growled. "There's been something between us since that first night. If you didn't want me, Laura, you wouldn't be so adamant about hanging on to your part of the business. Obviously, you don't know anything about it."

"I know everything there is to know about it, and wanting it has nothing to do with you!" Laura pressed herself into the corner of the couch, her principles not allowing her to get up and run as he edged dangerously nearer.

"Then why do I feel those golden eyes on me all the time?" His thigh came into contact with hers, and it felt like the scalding metal of a hot furnace.

"You don't!" she cried, but saw that he didn't believe her.

He insinuated his arm between the couch and her shoulders. "Give it up, Laura," he commanded softly, his mouth hovering a fraction of an inch from her lips. "Let's get this out of our systems."

Laura made a desperate push against his chest with both hands and gained enough freedom to ask, "Just what are you suggesting?"

"This, for starters." Ryder pulled her back against him, immobilizing her mouth with the hard pressure of his lips. Undaunted by her refusal to open her mouth to his searching tongue, he began a slow, gentle persuasion, tasting the corners of her lips as if he had all the time in the world. One steel-muscled arm swept around her back while his other hand cradled the back of her head, holding it still so his lips could move at will over her face.

Tiny kisses bestowed on her eyes, cheeks, and brow both tantalized and appeased her, but she wasn't completely willing to have the onslaught continue until he whispered gently in her ear, "Why do you make me say things I don't mean when all I want is to do this?" He kissed one eyelid. "And this." He kissed the other.

The ragged confusion in his voice melted something buried deep inside her, and all her resistance fled, replaced by the exciting knowledge that he could tap her inner depths like no other man. She needed to find out how deep he could go, if he could reach places she herself was not aware of.

She leaned toward him, moaning softly, allowing his tongue to slide inside her mouth where it abandoned all pretense of persuasion and dominated. She nestled closer, needing to feel his body against hers, wanting to feel the pleasure of her soft breasts flattened against the firm ridges of his chest. Her hands stole around to his back where her questing finger tips could run along the muscled width.

"You don't know how hard it's been to stay away from you these past two weeks," he rasped against her lips. A thorough exploration followed, his tongue delving in and around her mouth until she felt as if every crevice had been found and conquered. Burying his face in the hollow of her throat, he breathed deeply, then sighed. "God, you smell good. That luscious scent is everywhere in here, and it's been driving me crazy." Hungrily, his mobile lips wet a trail up her throat, nibbled at her jaw line, then devoured her lips in a consuming kiss that thrilled and captivated her senses.

Laura was eager to find out if she could cause a similar reaction in him. She returned his exploration with a daring one of her own, her tongue darting inside his mouth and evoking a tormented groan from deep inside him. Her hands moved across his back, kneading the muscles of his shoulders, sliding down his forearms, then up again to lock behind his neck. Her finger tips entwined in the thick black hair at his nape. While her hands moved over him, his were not idle, but slid down her shoulders, grasping her rib cage. He lifted her higher and tighter against him, his knuckles brushing the undersides of both breasts.

A shiver danced through her when his hand enclosed

the weighty fullness of one breast, the tips of his fingers sliding across the top edge of her dress. His mouth moved over her face, down her throat, and burned along the golden curves of her bosom as he pushed one strap, then the other, down her shoulders. His lips nudged the crisp fabric away from the twin prizes beneath, and his tongue encircled one taut nipple while his fingers imitated the action with the other.

"Ryder, this is crazy," she whispered desperately. "It'll only complicate things."

"No, it won't," he murmured huskily against her breast, continuing to moisten her erect nipple with the ministrations of his mouth.

"Please." She moaned, arching her body as she clutched her fingers in his hair.

His tortured sigh was both desperate and resigned. "We don't have to let it." Looking up, he caught her face between his large hands, and she could feel their trembling. "I want you, and you want me. I could take you right here, right now, but I'd prefer the luxury of one of those beds upstairs."

Laura did want him, wanted him with every fiber of her being. She could stop him, but maybe he was right. Maybe they did need to get this out of their systems before they could go on. Unwilling to spend another sleepless night fantasizing about him, she gave up. She would face the next day when it came.

At her hesitation, he dropped his hands away and leaned back. Not wanting to think about what she was doing, she stood up, holding her bodice with one hand. Reaching out, she caught Ryder's hand with the other. Her eyes were amber invitations that beckoned to him.

With increasing pleasure and an almost painful excitement, she read the rekindled hunger in his eyes as he came up off the couch in one coordinated motion. Barely able to withstand the intense blue promise of his gaze, she led the way up the stairs, hesitating at the top, unsure whether to go to her room or to his.

Sensing the reason behind her hesitation, Ryder opened the door to his room and drew her inside. He stood for a few seconds gazing into the gilded gray eyes that dominated her uptilted face, then slowly cradled her face in his hands and brushed her lips with his own. There was still a question in his kiss, and Laura answered by releasing the hold on her bodice and allowing her dress to slide to the floor.

She stood before him in nothing but bikini briefs, the golden girl he had described but no longer hiding anything.

"Laura," he said huskily, the accented tone more evident than ever in the soft drawling of her name, but this time there was no anger, only desire, a desire that exploded the instant he reached out for her. Between embraces, their clothing formed a trail across the floor as they moved toward the bed.

With one motion, Ryder swept aside the covers and lowered her onto the smooth cool sheets. His eyes swept across her tanned, naked body, illuminated by the stream of moonlight from the open windows. Laura surveyed the shadowed planes of his face, highlighted by the silvery light. Her nipples tightened as his gaze adored her golden curves. "You are so beautiful," he whispered, and slowly lowered himself on the bed.

Savoring the moment before their bodies would touch, she ran her eyes down the powerful torso poised over her. The strong lines of his body were devastating in the moonlight, more beautiful than that first night when she'd spied on him in the bathroom. This time, she could survey his entire body and didn't have to disguise her appreciation. Powerfully virile, totally aroused, he took her breath away. She opened her arms and welcomed his weight along her feverish length. Her sweet cries of pleasure as she returned his kisses mingled with the restless crashing of waves against the shore beneath their window.

Running his fingers into the wild mane that framed her face, Ryder commanded hoarsely, "Show me you want me, my lioness."

Spreading her fingers across his hair-clouded chest, her palms pressed against the hard flesh, reveling in the strength that must have taken years to build. More than willing to display her desire, she lifted her head from the pillow and started kissing his chest, flicking her tongue over the flat nipples that pricked her soft lips. She could feel the rapid throb of his heart beneath his heated bronze skin, and his involuntary shudders stoked her frenzy as she kissed him.

"No more." Ryder gasped, wrenching away and shifting his weight until his dark head rested between her heaving breasts. Tiny tremors shook her as his mouth took possession of one nipple, his tongue rasping against the sensitive peak that stood proudly erect, and her body arched rhythmically with the insistent pull of his demanding lips. Unable to withstand further onslaught of her senses, she opened her body to him, silently pleading for unity with his exquisite maleness.

She let him feel the writhing of her hips, sliding her hands down his sides to clutch the bunched muscles of his buttocks. She raised her hips to meet him, seductively challenging him with the enticing movement of her taut breasts, inflaming him by entwining her slender legs around his tensed thighs.

Full and heavy for her, he joined their bodies with a searing flash of fulfillment that portended a union as powerful as the highest wave on the shore. The upward spiral of pleasure swept them along until they hovered at the crest, swirling in a molten vortex of pleasure, then tumbling over in joyous wonder. Clinging to each other as the undertow of sensations ebbed and flowed, over and over.

Tangled together, their sweat-dampened bodies collapsed as one, their rapid breathing coming in halting gasps. To Laura, it seemed like hours before her breath slowed, and her arms and legs were tightly wound around Ryder's as she tried to grasp what had happened. When he withdrew from her, she felt as if a part of her had been taken away, and she moaned softly in protest.

"My God." Ryder groaned against her hair, his lips moving across her face as he kissed her softly, gently. Levering himself away from her until he lay on his side, he fingered the features of her face as he made love to her again with his eyes. "You are everything and more than I expected, golden girl."

"That doesn't sound like an insult this time," Laura murmured, still shaky in the aftermath of their coming together.

Burying his face in her hair, nuzzling her ear, he said whimsically, "Your hair, your bewitching golden eyes, and that glowing aura around you. You are a golden girl, and tonight you're mine." His warm breath fanned the sensitive skin behind her ear.

The muffled consonants, the soft inflection, and the fluid, rambling gallantry in his tone brought back the curiosity Laura had about him. "Where are you from,

Ryder? Sometimes you talk like you're from the East, but whenever you're angry or . . . or . . ."

"Making love?" He chuckled.

"Or making love, you have a southern accent. Why is that?" Turning over on her side, she propped herself up on one elbow and looked down at his face.

"I'm originally from Georgia," Ryder admitted, shrugging his shoulders as he pulled her down on top of his chest. "I didn't realize I did that, but I must revert when I'm not thinking about it. Or maybe you're the only one who can wipe out months of speech training. I'm not sure I like everything you do to me."

"I know a few things you like." Teasingly, Laura undulated her body, the tips of her breasts taunting the firm skin of his chest. Feeling his immediate reaction, she rolled away and dragged up a sheet to shield herself.

"Come back here, little lady." Ryder's accent was deliberately thick as he reached for her.

"Not until you tell me more." Laura giggled, slapping his hands away. "You know all about me, and I know nothing about you. That's not fair."

Grudgingly, he told her a little of his background— how he'd been raised on a small farm, left to join the army at eighteen, then struggled to erase any sign of his poor upbringing by taking lessons to refine his speech. It was an oddly defensive thing for him to have done, and she was surprised, but he explained that he'd lost several clients who had assumed his slow drawl also meant a slow brain.

"That's all you're getting tonight," he concluded gruffly, moving so swiftly that she was pinned beneath him before she could prevent it. He began nibbling an intoxicating line of kisses down her throat, and his expert hands drew lazy circles across her stomach. "I've developed this addiction, and you're the only one who can cure me."

His hands swept along the gentle curves of her hips and down the back of her legs, clasping her to him as he rolled them both over on the mattress until they were facing one another. "Am I?" She laughed, her finger tips whispering patterns over his back.

"Mmm." He stopped further conversation by bestowing a hard kiss on her waiting mouth. Searing kisses were pressed against warm, smooth skin until their caresses grew bolder. Mutual yearning drew their bodies together, both straining to intensify each sensation. They fitted concave to convex, soft to hard, male to female.

Entering her, Ryder lay still, only his hands sliding across her body as his mouth worked hers into motion. A warm liquid lethargy spread through Laura's lower body; then the tension built, and she moved against him, setting a rocking rhythm that Ryder couldn't resist. The pace gradually quickened until he swept her beneath him, his mouth never leaving hers. At the final climactic moment, he cried out her name.

Their floating recovery took longer this time, each wanting to hold on to the feelings, neither willing to end the experience with words. Nestled in his arms, she sailed dreamily along the smooth surface of utter fulfillment, alternately drowsing and waking to a renewed surge of tension that had to be satisfied. Sometime before dawn, they slept, exhausted and content in each other's arms.

8

Laura awakened slowly, not willing to let go of the delicious dream of being locked in Ryder's arms. As consciousness pushed the sleep away, she realized it wasn't a dream. Ryder's arms were still around her, his warm body pressed to her back as he cradled her against him. The significance of the night before overwhelmed her, and she knew that it had been a night of more than physical gratification. It had been a night of shared giving. Together, they had reached heights she hadn't known existed, found pleasure that went beyond the physical fulfillment they'd brought to one another. In one night, she'd reversed her opinion of him from an intruder who had completely disrupted her life to the man who enhanced the meaning of her life, the man she loved.

Reeling at the idea of falling in love with someone she barely knew, her sensible side warned her to slow down. What would Ryder do if she told him she loved him? She eased her body carefully away from his and turned on her side so she could look at his face. A slight smile turned up the corners of his mouth as if he were pleased with something. Was he dreaming of her as she had of him?

She memorized his features, loving his thick, sable lashes that formed dark crescents beneath his closed eyes, the rugged jaw that creased deeply whenever he smiled. Tenderly, she reached out with one finger and lightly traced the dark roughness that shadowed his cheeks, then leaned toward him and touched his lips with a whisper of a kiss.

She was about to draw back when a large hand clamped around the back of her head, effectively holding her in place. "And good morning to you, too." Ryder grinned, then brought her lips to his mouth.

When she was again allowed to breathe, she protested halfheartedly, "That was a sneak attack. I thought you were asleep."

"I haven't been asleep since you moved away from me. Besides, you fired the first shot. I was only retaliating." He chuckled, then compounded his reprisal with the entire arsenal at his disposal.

It was over an hour later before she was able to withdraw to the bathroom, take a hurried shower, then get ready for the trip Ryder had suggested for their first free morning together. As she stepped into the main part of the bathroom where Ryder stood wiping the remnants of shaving cream from his face, she went willingly into his arms, which folded her against a solid, masculine chest. He finally ended their heated exchange. "If we don't stop this, we'll spend the day in bed," he murmured against her lips, then lifted his head and grinned. "As enjoyable as that would be, I'd like to catch an early ferry so we'll have a full day on Kelly's Island."

"We could always take one of our boats over," she supplied hopefully.

"That sounds interesting." He grinned, boldly surveying her figure; then, as if stepping away from temptation, he backed off. "Humor me, Laura. Riding the ferry is a pleasure I've been looking forward to for weeks."

Laura didn't respond until she was safely beyond arm's length. "Seems there's been quite a few pleasures you've been looking forward to for weeks," she declared impishly.

"I'd say this weekend promises to fulfill all my dreams." He took a threatening step toward her, but she laughingly retreated to her bedroom.

The sun was shining brightly through her window, promising a warm day, and Laura chose her clothing accordingly. A teal-blue cotton shirt topped her oyster poplin split skirt. In deference to the cool breezes they would encounter aboard the ferry, she pulled on a pair of knee socks, then slipped her feet into comfortable loafers, knowing that Ryder's plans included a lot of walking. Brushing her hair away from her face into a ponytail, she secured it with a paisley scarf, then applied a light touch of shadow and mascara to her eyes. After outlining her lips with a coral gloss, she stood away from the mirror. Hurriedly, she stuffed a variety of items into a large shoulder bag, grabbed up her sweater, and hastened out of the room.

With Ryder at the wheel, they drove in Laura's convertible to Marblehead where they only had enough time before departure to eat a quick breakfast at a small fast-food drive-in. Once on board the ferry, they scrambled up the narrow stairs to the upper deck and took seats on a bench at the bow. The loud rumble of the powerful engine drowned out normal speech, and Laura was forced to shout as she directed Ryder's attention to the flock of gulls that gathered on the starboard side. She was rewarded by the sound of his laughter as he watched the normally graceful birds clumsily jockey for position as they dived for the bits of food tossed overboard by other passengers.

The bright sun had burned the morning fog off the lake's surface, which enabled them to see the misty outline of the island as the ferry cleared the pier. Although the lake was calm, they still felt the occasional spray of water dampening their clothes as they stood at the rail. Long before the ferry reached the island, they could discern the irregular shore line. Rocks and sand alternated with the thick stands of hardwood trees still in evidence despite the island's long history of lumbering. It was obvious that the early residents had had sufficient foresight to carefully harvest the oak, maple, and hickory that had once densely covered the land, but now dozens of vacation homes were snugly tucked between the towering trees.

Laura would have immediately disembarked, but Ryder became fascinated watching the cars being driven off the flat first deck onto the pier.

"I thought you were in a hurry to get started," she reminded, tugging on his hand.

"Okay, okay," he said but they didn't leave the boat until the assortment of trucks and cars were safely on shore.

Once on land, Ryder coerced her into falling in with another of his unexpected fantasies. Before she knew how he'd managed it, they were soon pedaling down the main road on an ancient tandem bicycle. Telling Ryder that the island was bigger than it looked had been in vain, for he was determined to explore its twenty-eight hundred acres at a leisurely pace under his own power.

"We should have brought the car," Laura wailed as they struggled up a slope in the road.

"We'll get the hang of it," Ryder remarked confidently. "As soon as we start working together. Are you pedaling?"

"Slowly, very slowly," she said breathlessly. "But I'll speed up if you promise to stop as often as I want."

"Is that a bribe?"

"Fair warning," Laura corrected him. "Otherwise, you might find yourself providing all the power for this thing. I haven't been on a bike in years."

"See what you've been missing?" He grinned over his shoulder, then let go of the handlebars. "Can't do this in a car."

"Ryder!" Laura squeaked as the bike began wobbling, but he immediately reclaimed control.

"Come on, Laura. Where's your sense of adventure?" He rounded a curve, increasing speed. "We'll enjoy the sights more this way, and we can both use the exercise."

"You sound like an ad for the bike-rental shop," she grumbled, hiding a smile. "Didn't you notice we were the only ones who rented a bike today?"

"Well, maybe we're the only tourists," Ryder suggested hopefully. "It looked like most of the other passengers were residents returning from the mainland."

"Lucky them," Laura intoned loudly, but Ryder

couldn't be swayed. He adjusted his pace to hers; after that, they rode in companionable silence until he turned in at one of the shops that dotted the lake-front village.

On display in the gift shop were the usual cedar boxes, printed T-shirts, and shell sculptures, but Ryder spied a hard-bound book about the history of the island and became engrossed while Laura continued browsing.

"See anything you want?" he asked, eventually rejoining her before a display of handmade Christmas ornaments.

Cradling a small wooden hobbyhorse, gaily decorated with a red and green plaid bow, Laura answered, "Yes, this."

"That's all?" he asked, turning his attention to the hand-carved ornament she held in her hand.

"Yes," she stated firmly. "It's not exactly representative of the island, but our family has always added a new, and preferably handmade, ornament to our Christmas tree every year." She paused, remembering that she'd be the only Davis celebrating the holidays that year.

Correctly interpreting her saddened expression, Ryder said quietly, "That's a tradition that should be carried on." His voice was sympathetic as they shared a moment of mutual understanding and loss, she for the grandfather she'd loved so deeply and he for the friend he'd respected and admired.

With their purchases safely tucked in a tote bag, they got back on their bicycle and headed toward the Kelly mansion, the most imposing structure on the island. The native limestone mansion, built during the Civil War, had been a wedding gift from Datus Kelly to his son Addison. Climbing the few steps to the pillared porch that extended around three sides of the building, Laura and Ryder paused to take in the same view of Lake Erie that generations of Kellys must also have enjoyed. Once inside, they were pleasantly greeted by the current owner of the mansion and encouraged to tour the building at their leisure.

One of the first things they noticed was the beautiful mahogany woodwork, lovingly maintained throughout the years. The original shutters, built inside the windows to protect the inhabitants from violent weather, were still in working order. "Look how they fold back into the woodwork when they're open," Ryder remarked, awed by the exquisite workmanship. "This kind of work can't be had today. I'll bet the Cliffs once had shutters like this."

"You'd be right," Laura agreed. "Beautiful, aren't they?" She pointed to the intricate plasterwork on the ceilings and the ornate chandeliers. "I'm sure I've seen fixtures similar to those up in our attic."

"Wouldn't you like having things like that around again?"

"I'd love it," Laura said enthusiastically. "Just look at that."

A circular staircase built of a solid piece of dark oak led upward past the second floor to the rotunda and widow's walk. Reciting from the brochure, Ryder informed her that the self-supporting structure, with its steps tied together in some mysterious fashion in groups of three, was one of only two in the world. The other staircase graced a house in London, England, and both had been built by the same craftsman. In order to preserve the beauty, the owners didn't allow anyone to use the staircase, so they climbed the back stairs, originally used by the house servants.

Touring the second floor, they were reminded of a time long past when the house would have been filled not only with family but with many guests, who would have occupied the numerous bedrooms built around the central balcony surrounding the staircase. Looking up, they could see the magnificent glass rotunda made of cobalt and ruby leaded glass. Unfortunately, they weren't allowed to ascend to the widow's walk, for the owner feared that someone might carelessly drop something that would shatter the priceless skylight that prismed light into beautiful patterns of blue and red.

Laura was sobered by the information that the mansion was no longer owned by the Kelly family but had been sold to the Dominican sisters of Adrian, Michigan, in 1933. It had been used as a retreat and education center for the sisters; then, in 1945, it opened as a summer camp for girls. In 1974, it had fallen into the hands of the present owners, who were diligently working to restore it. The comparison to the Cliffs was too close. Ryder already owned the greater portion of the estate, and Laura didn't like thinking it might someday pass entirely out of Davis hands.

She was silent as they toured the grounds, lost in thought. It was up to her to preserve the Davis legacy; no matter what Ryder planned, she wouldn't let him change things to suit himself.

"All this exercise has made me hungry. How about you?" Ryder asked, taking her arm and leading her toward the restaurant located alongside the mansion. He glanced at his watch and raised his eyebrows. "We were in there for nearly two hours. No wonder my stomach is growling."

Business was slow, and they had their choice of almost any table inside the dining room. They chose one by the windows that faced the lake and gave their orders to the waitress who had quickly appeared at their table.

Ryder grimaced when their orders arrived but waited until their waitress had departed before saying, "A lake full of perch and pickerel and the only food you can get is hamburgers, hot dogs, and fried chicken. Do you realize the only way someone can enjoy a fish dinner around here is to catch and cook the fish themselves?"

"It seems to be what the public wants," Laura remarked, missing his frown as she started eating her lunch.

Before continuing their bike ride around the island, they strolled across the narrow road to Inscription Rock. "Vandals got to this," Ryder said sadly, peering at the ancient petrographs.

"It's lucky the historical society stepped in when they did." Laura looked up from her brochure. "Those writings were made centuries before the white man came to this continent. According to this, Indians inhabited the island from 100 A.D. to 1654 A.D. The rock holds the secrets of their ancient ceremonies. Thank heavens someone cared enough to preserve it before it was lost forever."

"It's a shame someone didn't recognize its value before it was almost completely ruined," Ryder remarked as they started back across the street. "Unfortunately, it's human nature not to appreciate things until we're at the point of losing them."

Laura cast him a questioning look, but he was already on his way back to their bike. Was he trying to tell her something? She lost the opportunity to ask him if he was referring to something beyond Inscription Rock when he unsuccessfully attempted to wheel the unbalanced bike in a circle. He gestured to her empty seat. "Hop on, partner, or we won't be going anywhere."

They made their way toward the north side of the islands and the site of the famous glacial grooves. Occasionally, Laura would coast, which meant that Ryder was doing all the pedaling, but he discovered her inactivity going up a slight hill. "If you don't start pedaling, I'll set you down along the side, and you'll have to walk," he warned sternly, his eyes amused.

"I wasn't the one who insisted going miles under our own steam," she grumbled, but pumped her legs up and down in rhythm with his as she cursed the ancient coaster bike. "A ten-speed would have been nice."

"I like this one," Ryder called back over his shoulder.

"It probably reminds you of your truck," Laura sallied, shaking her head as Ryder laughed and began pedaling faster.

By the time they reached Glacial Groove Park, she'd never been so grateful to find evidence of the glacial period in her life. Her leg muscles were aching, and she was panting for breath. She was glad to see that Ryder was a bit winded himself as they viewed the remains of an abandoned limestone quarry.

"It's a perfect time to take your picture." Laura told him to stand by the protection rail overlooking the smooth limestone. "I want to remember you like this."

She thought his smile a bit stilted as she snapped the picture, but he didn't wait for her to request another pose. Looking down, then up, at the sky, he asked incredulously, "Can you imagine a sheet of ice two miles high? The mind boggles."

Laura found herself looking at the familiar sight with new eyes. "After seeing these old grooves so many times on school trips, I take them for granted. I guess they are pretty unusual, aren't they?"

Ryder placed his arm around her shoulders and pulled her close to his side as they descended the metal stairs. "Around here they aren't; not like some things."

Smiling up at him, Laura asked, "What things?"

"It's very unusual to find a golden-eyed blonde who feels so good in my arms." They'd reached ground level, and Ryder pulled her between his widespread legs as he lowered his head. It wasn't the quick kiss she expected but a slow exploration of her mouth.

When he lifted his lips away, she whispered, "Oh, Ryder, there's no one else who feels so good to me." She arched her body against him, completely forgetting where they were as her soft body encountered his heated strength and his mouth claimed hers again.

"Enough," he rasped, and pulled away. "Any more of this and we'll be rolling around in the bushes. It looks pretty secluded, but also full of poison ivy." They laughingly agreed that itching red welts would not be the best souvenir to take home from the island.

It was several more hours before they finally coasted down the last incline and returned the bike to the rental manager. By that time, they were hot, tired, and aching in every muscle. Starving, they had hoped to catch an outgoing ferry to get some dinner, but they had just missed it. "Can you stand eating another hamburger?" Ryder pointed down the road to a neon sign.

"I'll eat anything"—Laura bent down to rub her sore calves—"as long as I can sit down."

The return trip to the mainland was not as smooth as their first short voyage. Whitecaps foamed the rolling waves, and the plodding boat hit them full force as it followed its usual path directly to Marblehead. After a few minutes at the bow and a thoroughly cold drenching, Ryder and Laura elected to make the remainder of the trip in the safety of the cabin.

Once back at the house, they agreed to make it an early night. After her shower, Laura slipped into a jersey caftan and went downstairs. When she heard Ryder finish in the bathroom, she went into the kitchen to make some coffee.

Carrying a mug for each of them, Laura went back to the living room, pausing at the entrance. "Working?" she asked, surprised at seeing the open folder in Ryder's lap.

"Not really," he answered, closing the folder and placing it on the coffee table. "Just jotting down some ideas I gathered today." He accepted a mug from her and took a testing sip of the steaming liquid.

He stretched his arm along the back of the couch, and Laura curled up in the inviting spot next to him. "We never got around to discussing business last night. Do you want to explain your proposals to me now?"

He sipped his coffee, then placed his mug down on the table. Extending his hand, he took her cup and set it down next to his. With his free arm, he switched off the brass-shaded lamp. "I'd rather not discuss any business tonight." He pulled her across his lap and settled her head against his shoulder. "My partner, the formidable Miss Davis, went away for the weekend, didn't you know? A warm, delectable woman is here in her place." His lips moved across her forehead, and his hand moved lightly up and down her arm, sending delicious shivers along her spine. The faint rustle of material as her caftan slithered beneath his touch was the only sound in the room, and Laura relaxed in the comfortable shelter his body provided.

She breathed deeply of the scent of his recently showered body, a mixture of soap and the light, tangy aftershave he always wore. "You know, that aftershave of yours nearly drove me crazy. It was the only clue I had that you had been in the house during the last two weeks. I was beginning to think you weren't human."

"Maybe too human," he muttered, then lowered his lips to hers. She opened to him, her soft lips urging his tongue's invasion and her hand moving to the back of his head to press him closer. Her tongue made an invasion of its own, the tip dancing along the inside of his mouth until he groaned. In one smooth motion, Ryder stretched them both along the couch, and Laura welcomed his long length against her.

Ryder's wandering hand found the long slit at the side of her caftan; immediately, his palm was smoothing the silken skin of her thighs. Impatient with the barrier his shirt made between her hands and his flesh, Laura pulled it from his trousers, then spread both palms in a circular pattern across his broad, muscled back. She ran her finger tips down the indentation of his spine, then teased a short distance under the waistband of his trousers.

Ryder responded in kind by inserting his finger tips just inside the elastic of her bikini briefs, sending ripples of reaction along her flat stomach until Laura writhed against him. "This wasn't the place last night, nor is it tonight," he managed between ragged breaths, and rolled off the couch onto his feet in one synchronized motion. He reached out his hand to pull her up. "Come on upstairs, unless you'd prefer the floor." He started toward the hall, her hand held tightly in his.

There was no hesitation that night; he led her immediately into his room and started unbuttoning his shirt while Laura reached for the hem of her caftan and pulled the garment over her head. Her slippers and briefs swiftly joined the caftan on the floor. Moving to the bed, Laura pulled back the covers, stretched out on the mattress, and watched with growing fascination as Ryder peeled off his remaining garments. The partially obscured moon dusted the room with pale light, barely outlining Ryder's muscular body. It was enough light to discern his smooth flesh from the shadowed hair on his torso, and she felt her body tighten, remembering how that hair had tantalized her flesh the night before.

The mattress dipped with his weight, and Laura rolled toward him. Her hands were drawn to his neck, and she ran her finger tips along the corded muscles that led to his wide shoulders. Ryder wrapped one arm around her and pressed close to her body, fitting her curves against his hard planes, capturing her mouth with his. Soft moans erupted from her throat as his tongue conquered hers and plundered the sweet recesses of her mouth. His tongue continued its passionate assault, trailing down her throat, encircling first one aching nipple, then the other.

As his mouth fastened on her breast, Laura arched against him and ran her hands down his muscle-roped sides until she reached his hips, where she pulled him closer. A wave of rapture flooded her body when she felt the heated hardness of his need for her pressing against her supple thighs. He slid farther down her body, his hands and mouth stimulating her with agonized pleasure. With a shuddering gasp, she welcomed his intimate torture of her throbbing desire, and her body undulated seductively, her legs moving restlessly. He brought her to the brink of fulfillment again and again, the flames of her ecstasy rising higher with each stroke of his tongue, until at last she cried out her need for him.

He answered her impassioned plea by moving his lips back up her body. Positioning himself between her thighs, he prolonged the moment before the most intimate of embraces by making a gentle foray of her with his finger tips. He guided her hand until she closed around him and returned his stroking rhythm. "Oh, sweet love," he whispered as the fury of his arousal reached the same plateau as hers. She guided them to complete unity, and they moved together toward fiery consummation. Ryder collapsed on her, and their breathing was a long time returning to normal. Nestling his head in the curve of her shoulder, he pressed soft kisses along her throat while they made their slow descent from the heated zenith.

Eventually, he rolled to his side, turned her toward him, and pillowed her head on his shoulder, his hand resting on her hip. "That was the best business I ever conducted with a partner," he mumbled before falling asleep.

Laura lay contentedly in the warm circle of his arms, enjoying the steady rise and fall of his chest beneath her palm. Suddenly feeling chilled despite the warmth emanating from Ryder, she moved her hand down his body, stopping to spread her fingers through the tantalizing hair that spread across his muscle-hardened flesh, then reached for the edge of the covers and pulled them up to enclose both of them in the comfortable nest of the bed. Her eyelids closed, and she felt herself drifting off to join Ryder in the blissful slumber of aftermath when the meaning of his last words assailed her and her eyes flew open.

"Business with a partner?" She tried to move away

from him, but his arms tightened around her, and she was forced to remain where she was. She replayed the events of the day over and over in her mind.

She remembered his seemingly teasing remark about the "formidable Miss Davis." Formidable, was she? Was that why he didn't want to talk about the changes that night and effectively silenced any argument she might have made about discussing his proposals by making love to her. Was the incredible experience they'd just shared been a business maneuver? I'll just bet it was the best business he ever conducted with a partner, she fumed, and fought the temptation to wake him with a punch in the stomach and have it out then and there. The only reason she didn't was because she wanted to be in complete control when she confronted him with her accusations.

She was far too attracted to him, easily aroused by him, to maintain her composure if they had it out in their present setting. All he'd have to do is sweep her back into his arms and kiss her into submission until she forgot all her suspicions. Scarlett O'Hara, you may have had a good philosophy, Laura mused bitterly. Some things are better thought about tomorrow. But her fears continued to torment her, and she was unable to sleep. Eventually, she slipped out of the bed and crept quietly to her own room. There was no way she could comfortably go to sleep at his side until she was sure of his feelings.

9

~~~~~~~~~~~~~~

Standing under the warm spray of the shower, Laura lathered her body with a soapy sponge. She could still feel Ryder's caresses; the scent of his body clung to hers until she'd scrubbed every inch and shampooed her hair, but she could not wash away her growing doubts about Ryder's motives. Had their weekend together only been a means to an end? He wanted no interference, and perhaps he thought their time together had erased any thoughts she might have had about blocking his future plans for the inn. For some reason, he'd switched the subject every time she'd mentioned the changes he planned to make, and she'd been so swept away by her feelings for him that she hadn't pursued it.

He was a superb lover; she'd never experienced anything so wondrous with another man. In fact, she'd never spent an entire weekend making love and opened herself so completely to a man. After the first night, she'd considered herself in love with him and had hoped he loved her, too, but love had to be based on more than physical attraction, and she refused to accept her feelings toward Ryder as love when she feared he might only have been using her to get what he wanted. His words came back to her, tormenting her. "I hope to fulfill all my dreams this weekend." Was a short-lived affair with her one of those dreams, or did he have more in mind?

Stepping out of the shower, she toweled herself dry and slipped into her robe. Back in her room, she chose a pair of cream-colored slacks and a deep loden-green blouse before noiselessly making her way down the stairs to the kitchen. She was relieved when she'd tiptoed past Ryder's door to find that he was still asleep. She needed some time to herself before facing him that morning.

She knew the refrigerator had little to offer other than orange juice. Having eaten most of their meals at the inn, she'd done little shopping since her arrival. Remembering the small market within a mile of the Cliffs, she grabbed her purse and keys and quietly let herself out the kitchen door.

Driving the short distance inland to the market, she was aware of the change in temperature. During the night, a cold front had moved in from the north, one of the first signs that autumn was at hand. Summers didn't linger along the lake; they were chased away by cold Canadian breezes that scudded over the Ohio shore, intermittently reminding the inhabitants of the winter to come. Brilliant chrysanthemums bloomed in many of the yards she passed, representing the last stand of the growing season. A few leaves were already beginning to turn on the hardwoods, burnished highlights amid the green. There was a sharp edge in the tangy air that heralded the unrelenting approach of biting cold, months of white, frozen silence that would crash to an end when the massive chunks of ice would finally be broken by the insistent rays of the spring sun.

Laura wondered what winter would bring for her. Would it be a warm, loving time shared by her and Ryder, or would they drift apart like the floes of ice that melted, then disappeared beneath the cold waters of the lake each spring? Their relationship was still too new for her to have answers, and she tried not to think about it as she drove the remaining distance inland.

At the market, Laura pushed her cart through the aisles of fresh fruit and vegetables. She smiled to herself, thinking of meals to prepare that couldn't be had at the inn's restaurant. No more fried chicken, greasy hamburgers, or even the ordinary breakfasts of bacon and eggs! With her taste buds crying out for anything that wasn't grilled or deep-fried, she filled her cart with the ingredients she'd need for her planned breakfast.

Once back at the house, she quickly emptied the grocery bags, slipped into the apron Ryder had worn that first morning, and went to work. She prepared a creamy hollandaise sauce to be spooned over delicately poached eggs and served with thick slices of hot Canadian bacon. When Ryder appeared at the kitchen door, freshly showered and clean-shaven, aromatic coffee was dripping in the coffee maker. She was so engrossed in splitting English muffins in for the toaster that she didn't hear him come in.

She gasped when warm hands slipped around her waist and a familiar growl tingled her ear. "Whatever you're making smells almost as good as you do." Ryder kissed her neck, nibbled up the cord at the side of her throat, and nuzzled her ear until she couldn't stand the shivering sensations coursing along her spine.

"You're distracting the cook," she protested, laughing as he dropped his hands and gazed longingly over her shoulder.

"Thank God that's not bacon or sausage," he intoned with relief. "You must be as sick of restaurant food as I am."

"So don't bother me or the muffins will burn," she ordered, pulling down the lever on the toaster.

"If I wasn't so hungry, I'd take the chance." Ryder grinned, his dimples forming attractive craters beside his mouth. "Carry on, sweet chef."

After planting a light kiss on her cheek, he crossed the kitchen and poured himself a cup of coffee. "I didn't even hear you get out of bed this morning. How early did you get up?"

"With the birds." Laura breathed a soft sigh of relief. He had no idea that she had left him during the night and gone to her own room. Composing her features, she motioned for him to sit down, and he leisurely took his seat at the table.

She was puzzled over the clothes he was wearing. His dark sport coat and light dress pants didn't indicate a casual day at the Cliffs, but she couldn't recall his offering another invitation and decided that his plans didn't include her.

Turning back to the counter, Laura tried unsuccessfully to keep her attention on the task of arranging poached eggs and smoked meat on the muffin rounds before carefully spooning the sauce over the top, for she was very aware that Ryder's eyes were quietly but steadily roaming over her figure. She was growing increasingly unsure of his feelings but couldn't doubt his desire. Now that he'd spent a weekend making love to her, would he expect to share her bed every night? What kind of arrangement did he have in mind? One that involved commitment or one that was merely to get their mutual attraction out of their systems? Wasn't that what he had told her he planned to do Saturday night? It certainly had not worked out that way for her, but she wondered if their passion-laden nights had satisfied his desire for her. She dismissed that notion at once. His eyes were systematically undressing her, electric-blue scanners reflecting his appetite for something more than a home-cooked breakfast.

Yet that morning she'd had the time to consider the consequences of what she was doing and what she was inviting for the future. What would Tom say if he knew that she and Ryder shared a bed as well as the house? Then there were Sophie and Will. Even though it appeared that they had switched their allegiance from her to Ryder, they had been like a second set of grandparents to her, and she doubted they would understand their sleeping together without the sanctity of marriage. Marriage? Ryder had given no indication that he wanted a lifelong commitment. Indeed, she was beginning to think he'd already achieved what he wanted from her. Perhaps the only goal he had left was to get the changes he wanted underway before ending their affair.

Hiding her uncertain suspicions, she crossed the room and placed the eggs Benedict on the table in front of Ryder. Sitting down, she avoided Ryder's eyes and began to eat while the tension built up inside her. Unaware of his increasingly puzzled expression, Laura ate her breakfast, not offering any conversation.

Ryder followed suit, but when he had finished, he pushed back his plate, folded his arms on the table, and leaned forward, demanding, "Out with it, Laura."

Shifting uneasily in her seat, Laura couldn't disregard the unblinking command in his dissecting eyes. "I guess I'm not sure where we go from here," she admitted, searching his face.

He appeared to have difficulty interpreting her expression, frowning as he inspected the bluish tinges under her overbright gray eyes, the unnatural paleness beneath the golden tan of her face. Then he seemed to make up his mind about something. His lips went tight. "Didn't take you long to have second thoughts, did it?" Ryder raised both arms and clasped them behind his neck, massaging the skin beneath his hairline. "When I found you in here acting like the happy homemaker, I thought you wanted what's happened between us as much as I did. I haven't been this relaxed since I first laid eyes on you, but this weekend seems to have had the opposite effect on you. You're as nervous as a cat this morning."

So he was relaxed, was he? Laura wanted to ask if his relaxation was caused by the warm euphoria of new love or simply the release from sexual tension. She didn't like his describing her as a complacent housewife who was joyfully content with her lot because he satisfied her needs in bed and became even more certain she was right to mistrust him. "I'm not nervous, Ryder, but I am thinking about the future. Do you want us to go on living together?"

When he didn't look at her but stared at a spot over her head, her distrust increased further. "I thought I'd made it very clear what I want. Living together is a quaint expression that hardly covers what we've been doing. What do you want, Laura?" Before she could answer, he added, "Besides me?"

"I want a lot of things," she said, hating the flush that burned in her cheeks. "But what I don't want is a short-term affair with you. It's very convenient for you, I'm sure, but I don't gain anything, do I?"

Not like you, she silently cried, praying he'd deny her fear and tell her his emotions were as deeply involved as hers. It was agony not to scream when he continued in a casual tone that implied he didn't care about anything but the future of the inn and satisfying his physical needs.

"It's essential that I be on hand to oversee all the construction that will be going on." Ryder stared out the window at the view of the lake beyond. "And it would be the practical solution to everything if we continue as we are. I'd like nothing more than to go on as we have this weekend, but it doesn't sound as if you want that. Sounds like all I gained was two enjoyable nights. I'd hoped for more."

"I'm sure you did," Laura exclaimed contemptuously, so hurt she lashed out. "But that's all it was."

She died a little inside when he shrugged. "So, in the future, I'll restrain my lust." He sat up straighter in his chair and impaled her with his eyes. "Don't worry, I'll keep my distance. I just hope you can do the same."

If he was capable of keeping his distance from her, then his feelings weren't involved, and she'd never admit she'd thought herself in love with him. He couldn't have made it more clear that he would be satisfied with an occasional romp in the bedroom, but she yearned for so much more. Shifting her gaze away from the icy-blue shroud he was casting over her with his eyes, she struggled for control. "I don't plan to have any trouble on that score." She decided to go a step further and prove she could be as practical about the situation as he. "Since you have to be near the inn, I'll look for an apartment."

Ryder smacked his hand down on the table, making her jump. "Don't be ridiculous! If you're worried about what people might say, I'll make it perfectly clear that all we're doing is coresiding under the same roof. This is a fairly good sized house, and we're both adults. I can control my baser instincts. If you recall, I've never attacked you. You enjoyed it as much as I did. I promise you it won't happen again until you say you want it." There was something forced about his voice, and she was certain he was deliberately controlling his accent.

"Are you saying two days was enough to get everything out of our systems?" She refused to back down under his scathing expression.

"Not everything, Laura." Ryder stood up and glanced at his watch as if he didn't have any more time to devote to such unimportant matters. "I've got an appointment with Lou Parisi at the Château de Vin Isle. I'm trying to work out a deal with him to feature the local wines in the new dining room I'm going to build."

"What new dining room?" Laura gasped, stung by the note of dismissal in his voice. "Is that one of these mysterious changes you've been planning?"

"It is."

"Which you never mentioned all weekend."

"I got sidetracked, and there's a lot I didn't mention." He rounded the table and started for the door. "If you want to read through the folder I left on the desk in the living room, we can discuss everything when I get back from my meeting with Lou."

"We'll discuss everything right now!" Laura demanded, standing up from her chair.

Her answer was a resounding slam of the door as Ryder walked out on her. Running across the room, Laura tore open the door, but wasn't in time to catch him. She was left standing on the stoop in impotent rage as he started his truck and sped down the graveled drive. A cloud of dust from his spinning wheels settled over her head, choking her, irritating her eyes, but the tears coursing down her cheeks were caused more by hurt and rage than by the swirling grit.

Twenty minutes later, Laura was still struggling with the dirty dishes. She had scoured the bottom of a copper frying pan until it shone more brilliantly than it had in years, stopping only when she saw her angry reflection on the smooth metal bottom. "And who on earth is Lou Parisi?" she shouted at the cooling water in the sink, throwing down her dishrag as she began putting the dried glassware in the cupboards.

She recalled everything she knew about the château, which had stood for more than a century on the peninsula. The small winery, owned for generations by the Duvall family, had never produced any large quantity of wine. In recent years, the Duvalls had concentrated on running a small restaurant above the winery, catering to a select clientele. As far as she knew, the château produced only enough wine to be served on the premises, and she wondered what kind of deal Ryder could possibly make when the quantities were so limited.

Had another family business fallen into the grasping hands of a brash newcomer? If Parisi had the right to make deals, he had to be the owner, but she'd never heard of him and wondered what had happened to the elderly Duvalls. More importantly, what kind of grandiose plans had Ryder conceived that would require an association with a premier winemaker? Unless Parisi was considering the expansion of his vineyards. Was Ryder contemplating selling a portion of Davis land to Parisi? If so, he would never get her approval.

She dispelled that idea as rapidly as the thought had formed. He had mentioned making a deal that involved a new dining room at the Cliffs. Therefore, he must be negotiating a purchase of château wines. If so, he had to be envisioning quite an elegant restaurant, as Château de Vin Isle was known for producing wines of the very finest quality, though in small quantity. Such an idea was idiotic! The Cliffs' grill had served their patrons adequately for years, and there was no need for a fancier facility at the family resort.

Her mind raced with all the changes that might result from this possibility, and she hurried through the remainder of the kitchen cleanup chores, anxious to get at the folder containing all Ryder's ideas. Maybe after she'd looked them over, she'd have some conception of where things were going. She had to be sensible, to get all the facts before trying to prevent any changes.

Seething inside, she realized what Ryder had been doing all weekend. The purpose behind his subtle comments about food, atmosphere, and restoration were now glaringly apparent. He'd shrewdly laid the groundwork for getting her agreement without her knowing where it would lead. Worse, he thought his expertise as a lover might soften any future opposition on her part. Well, at least she had the satisfaction of knowing he hadn't accomplished that goal. She was more determined than ever to stand in his way.

In a momentary flash of self-honesty, she admitted that she'd done absolutely nothing to discourage him in the bedroom. She had made love to him with no ulterior motives in mind; obviously, he had not. The memory of her unbridled responses to his intimate stroking filled her with self-loathing. "Ryder Bantel, you're a double-dealing snake! I was a fool to fall for that southern charm!" She slammed a cupboard door to enunciate her words, but it flew back open in her face, making her even more angry. She gave it a vicious backhand, bruising her knuckles. "Blast it! Stay shut."

"Haven't heard you yelling in the kitchen for a long time." Sophie came through the back door. "I did knock, but you didn't hear me."

Sheepishly, Laura turned around. "I had someone else in mind."

"I gathered that," the white-haired woman said, her snapping blue eyes alight with mirth, "Ryder?"

"I know you and Will think he's wonderful, but I have my doubts." Laura sank into the nearest chair, exhausted from her tirade.

"What did he do, honey?" Sophie inquired, her lips twitching.

Hesitating, Laura strove for an even tone. "It's not what he's done, it's what he's planning to do. Has he mentioned a new dining room to you, Sophie?"

"Yes, he has." Sophie surprised Laura with supplying an affirmative answer, as if the older woman assumed that Laura probably knew about it, too. "We've been needing a good restaurant around here for years. Folks have to go too far for something a little different. You know that old house over there'd be the perfect setting for what Ryder has in mind. Why, when I was a girl . . ." Sophie began what Laura knew from past experience could become a lengthy, rambling description of how much better things were in the past.

"When the Cliffs was still the Davis family mansion, there was no grander place around here. It'll seem like old times to have crystal chandeliers, fine linen, and good wines served to gracious, well-dressed people who know the difference between hamburger and Chateaubriand.

"It was Prohibition that brought an end to the good old days. I'm glad there's some young people left who can envision the way things used to be. Ryder's bringing back some old traditions that would've made your grandpa, rest his soul, proud."

"Traditions?" Laura jumped on the word, hoping Sophie would stop long enough for her to have her say. When it looked as though that wouldn't happen, Laura held up her hands in supplication. "Gramps wouldn't want any such thing! He always said the Cliffs was meant to be enjoyed by families. We don't cater to the rich, never have. Ryder's been telling me how badly we're doing, then turns right around and wants to throw good money away on a crazy proposition like this. It'll never work."

"Sure it will," Sophie asserted. "He convinced me and Will right along with your grandfather the first few days he was here. If you can't trust Ryder's judgment, you should trust your grandfather's. He gave Ryder free rein."

"Well, he's certainly taken it." Laura fumed, sensing that there was no way she could convince Sophie that Ryder was in the wrong. She certainly couldn't disclose that he'd seductively used her to get his own way. She was ashamed enough of that as it was!

"Have you looked at the proposals Ryder's worked up?" Sophie asked, sternly pinning Laura with a penetrating stare. Seeing Laura's guilty expression, she admonished, "Laura Davis, you weren't brought up to make snap judgments. What's really bothering you, Laura, Ryder's plans or the man himself?"

Laura had that to think about for the rest of the day. After Sophie had left, she sat down with the folder and tried to digest the projections Ryder had proposed. As she studied them, she realized that not only was Ryder planning to construct another dining room; he would be doubling the facilities for overnight guests. She couldn't imagine what kind of costs would be involved and how he could justify such outrageous plans in the face of their declining profits. His recommendations would change the entire complexion of the present building and attract a completely different type of clientele. He even suggested the inn be kept open all year round!

Snapping the folder shut, Laura began to pace around the room. He's a fool! she judged silently. How could he possibly imagine they'd draw enough business to keep the inn open all year? The building wasn't presently adequate for year-round use, and the cost of heat and insulation would be astronomical. Surely, if he intended to make renovations of such magnitude, he'd have to get her approval. He might own the major percentage of the property, but her forty-nine percent share gave her some power.

If he went bankrupt on the deal, so would she. He might be a successful manager, an experienced hotel consultant, but he didn't know the area as she did, and what he was proposing couldn't possibly be successful.

She did give him credit for coming up with a tasteful idea, not the garish monstrosity she'd envisioned, but even so, it was far too grandiose for the area.

Knowing he deemed her so gullible, she'd let his lovemaking cloud her business judgment, and that caused a sharp pain in her heart. He had never had any intention of explaining a thing, hoping she'd become emotionally tied to him and agree to anything he suggested.

Soon he'd find out that no matter what kind of personal relationship they had, she'd stick by her convictions. She knew the county commissioners wouldn't readily approve the massive upgrade necessary to increase the Cliffs' water supply and waste disposal. The work involved would be extremely expensive, and the inn would have to absorb the assessments. She questioned whether Ryder had taken that into consideration. To bring the new facility Ryder devised up to code would entail the cooperation of all the utilities. Perhaps she wouldn't have to do anything to stop him herself. He was going to be involved in a lengthy battle with the city fathers that might take years to resolve. Maybe, when he'd butted his head against a stone wall long enough, he'd give up, sell her his interest, and move on. Wouldn't that make life easier for everyone?

Her life had been so much simpler before Ryder had stepped in. But she could live without his kisses, the sound of his drawling voice, the feel of his arms around her, couldn't she?

She shook her head. She'd had to fight against her attraction to him from the first night when he'd assisted her inside his rattletrap truck on the Old Harbor Road— his body a visual treat she now craved with everything in her, his complex personality a constant challenge she yearned to confront daily. He'd become a part of her life long before he'd entered her bed. One part of her wished he'd never come back, but another part, her emotional self, desired to throw herself in his arms and beg him to make love to her as soon as he walked through the door.

10

~~~~~~~~~~~~~

Ryder swept back into the house like a whirlwind, the exhilarated expression on his face in total contradiction to the black scowl he'd worn when he'd left that morning. He strode toward Laura, who was standing by the bay window in the living room, looking as if he'd forgotten every angry word they'd spoken earlier. When he reached her, he lifted her off her feet, twirled her around, then planted a brief, hard kiss on her astonished mouth. "Sorry about that"—his grin was unabashed as he set her down—"but Lou and I have finally got everything set. We want to celebrate. Go get changed. We're meeting the Parisis at the Shore House for dinner."

He appeared not to notice her wiping her mouth with the back of her hand as he ordered, "Let's get going. We've only got forty-five minutes."

"I'm not going anywhere," she fumed, digging in her

heels as he neatly tucked her arm beneath his and started edging her toward the stairs. "Let go of me."

"We'll talk things over on the way," he promised, forcing her to move.

Since he was so much stronger than she was, there was little she could do to stop him from strong-arming her, but she refused to go willingly. "I don't want any part of Parisi, or you!"

Sensing he was about to hoist her over his shoulder as they reached the bottom of the stairs, she reached out and made a desperate grab for the rail. "I won't stand for this, Ryder."

"Do you want to find out what's going on, or don't you?" Ryder inquired, his expression bland.

"Of course, but not this way," she exclaimed adamantly. "I'm not being bulldozed into anything."

"I'm not bulldozing you." Ryder reached for her hand, gripping the rail. "This is as much your celebration as mine. I want you there, partner. Lou's bringing his wife. I'm bringing you. You'll like Lou and Maria. They're great people."

Before surrendering to the firm pressure being applied on her wrist, Laura ranted. "I won't like anyone who agrees with your insane proposals. As far as I'm concerned, he's another outsider who thinks he knows more about our business than people who've lived here all their lives. I've spent the entire day reading your far-fetched ideas, and I don't approve of a single one. Even if you could find the money to make those kind of changes, they'd never—"

"I'm in too good a mood to argue with you," Ryder exclaimed exuberantly, placing her in a far more dangerous position than the one she'd been in before. With a fast downward motion of his hand, he broke her grip on the rail, then lifted her up in his arms. She gasped as he let go of her, then caught her again in an all-encompassing hold that adjusted her body more closely against his. His mouth took hers in a devastating kiss that lasted all the way up the stairs. Placing her down before her bedroom door, he advised, "Hurry up."

"Listen!" Laura sputtered. "I've never heard of these people and wouldn't want to meet them even if I did." Her breasts were still tingling from being crushed against him, and she crossed her arms over her chest, unprepared to deal with both her reactions to his kiss and her feelings about the Parisis at the same time.

"They've heard a lot about you." Ryder reached around her and opened her bedroom door.

"From who?" she inquired shortly.

"From me." Ryder grinned, unmoved by her black mood. "I told them you were a prime example of the kind of stubborn opposition we can expect around here. Set in your ways, stubborn, and totally illogical."

"You didn't!" Laura screeched, appalled.

"If you want to prove me wrong, go get dressed," Ryder suggested, turning her around and prompting her to enter her room by delivering a light swat to her bottom.

By the time she'd whirled back to face him, he was halfway down the hall. "I also said you were beautiful," he said soothingly, then stepped inside his room and shut the door.

Laura took several huge swallows of air and counted to ten. Don't let him get away with this, she ordered herself, finally attaining enough control to close her door without breaking it off the hinges. She would prove something all right, prove she could separate her personal and business affairs. She'd meet the Parisis, charm the socks off them, and show everyone just how logical she could be. She had a good argument against every point Ryder had raised in his reports, and by the end of the evening, she'd have him looking like a fool for describing her to the Parisis as he had.

Knowing she needed every advantage she could get, she chose to wear an elegant blue silk shirtwaist. Draping it carefully over the chair near the closet, she went to her dresser and pulled out a pair of blue bikini panties and a matching demicup bra. After changing into the undergarments, she stepped into a satin half-slip, then drew on silk hose and placed her feet into dainty sling-back pumps.

Sitting at the vanity, she carefully applied her make-up, then arranged her blond curls in a sophisticated upswept style that accentuated the size of her eyes. She applied a delicate scent to her throat, wrists, and breasts, just replacing the glass stopper back in the perfume bottle when she heard a sharp knock.

"Ready?" Ryder inquired from the other side of her door.

"Not yet," she sang, saccharine dripping from each syllable. "Let him wait," she stated smugly to her reflection in the mirror.

"What's holding things up?" Ryder inquired, stepping into the room without warning. He strolled toward her, casually shoving his hands into the pockets of his slacks.

Swiveling around, Laura stood up to order him out of her room but caught her heel in the carpet, lost her balance, and began falling. His arms were there before she reached the floor, pulling her breathless form against his crisp cotton shirt, navy sportcoat, and gray flannel slacks. Feeling very vulnerable in her underwear, she twisted in his arms, but his face was buried in the tumble of curls atop her head, and he wouldn't let go of her.

"Why do you always smell so damned good?" he inquired thickly, lowering his lips to the tender skin beneath her ear, then trailing hungry kisses down her throat. His hands slid over her bare midriff, coming to rest around her slender waist as he brought her lower body against his thighs.

"Don't," she pleaded halfheartedly, trying to withstand the delicious shivering that followed the tantalizing movement of his lips working across her shoulders.

"No?" The tender question was coupled with a hand softly stroking the full curve of her breast.

"No," she murmured, parting her lips for his kiss. His tongue answered her provocative invitation by exploring deeply, seeking the sweetness she'd reserved for him alone, even as her own tongue delved into his mouth, relearning what tiny motions gave him the most pleasure.

His low, muffled growls of need filled her with an overwhelming sense of womanly power, and she began unbuttoning his shirt. Sliding her hands inside, she smoothed her finger tips over his warm flesh in the tormenting way she knew he liked, melting against him as his kiss hardened with demand.

Before she knew how it happened, she found herself reclining on the bed, her breasts bared. Ryder leaned over her, cupping her breasts with both hands as his mouth claimed each nipple in turn. Her fingers clutched in his dark hair, pulling his head to her as she felt the tremors build up inside her. Needing him, she tugged at his arms, breathing unsteadily as he slid himself up the mattress and confiscated her lips.

Frantically, she tugged at his shirt, pulling it loose from his slacks so her hands could roam the copper expanse of naked skin she'd uncovered. His kisses added to the magical sorcery of his knowing touch, enslaving her senses, exposing her need. When his lips were removed, her eyes flew open with alarm, but he placed two fingers over her mouth and gazed lovingly into her eyes. "Be patient, my lioness. We'll save this for later. Right now we need to get going."

Laura shut her eyes, unable to comprehend how she'd allowed herself to succumb to him yet again. Fool! Fool! she screamed silently, taking a shattered breath as she fought for control. She grabbed his wrist and shoved his hand away. "There won't be a later," she cried softly, opening her eyes to stare up at him. "I didn't want this. I didn't." Her words sounded more as if she were trying to assure herself than him.

"Who undressed whom?" Ryder challenged tenderly, his dimples twin hollows of amusement.

"You promised not to touch me," she reminded, too distraught to think about his likely response to such a leading remark.

He got off the bed, holding her eyes in a blue snare as he slowly began rebuttoning his shirt. She could see that he was trying to decide whether or not to call her on her foolish words and knew the second he'd made his decision. "Pull in your claws, sweetheart. We'll talk about what you want later. Right now, we're late. I'll meet you downstairs in fifteen minutes."

Laura dragged a sheet over her nakedness. "I'm not going anywhere with you. After what you've done, I . . . I . . . ."

"Are you or are you not my business partner?" Ryder demanded, looking back from the doorway.

"That has nothing to do with it," Laura shot back.

"That has everything to do with it." Spying her dress on the chair, he strode back into the room, picked it up, and tossed it smoothly on the bed. "Tonight or never, Laura. I want you to know what's going on."

"Sure." She wouldn't look at him. "That's why you stormed out of here this morning. That's why you've made a deal with a man I've never met—because you're so anxious for my approval."

He rubbed the heel of his hand over his forehead, then said angrily, "I didn't take you with me this morning because I was too damned mad to think straight. Last night, we shared something wonderful; this morning, you tell me it's over. What the hell was I supposed to do, grin and bear it? I'm a man, Laura, and I've got as many needs as you do."

"Do you?" Her expression was doubtful. "If so, I know exactly what they are. You used me this weekend, made love to me to postpone discussing the future of the Cliffs. You took me on that trip to the island just to trick me into agreeing with some of your plans." She mimicked his low voice. "Can't find a decent meal around here, Laura. Don't you like these shutters? Wouldn't it be great if you'd agree to everything I want without making any more waves?"

"Is that what you think?" His features were frozen, an ashen tinge beneath his tan.

"It's what I know."

He turned away as if the sight of her sickened him. Without looking back, he strode toward the door. "Get dressed. I'd call Lou and beg off, but he's probably already waiting for us at the restaurant. I promised we'd be there, and we will."

His accent was pronounced, and she was compelled to exclaim, "Why should he count on one of your promises? They don't mean anything."

Deadly blue eyes pinned her to the bed. "I told you once I won't tolerate any interference in the business. Do you want me to prove right now how far I'll go if you keep this up?"

A bubble of panic lodged in her throat. He looked capable, almost eager, to commit violence as he waited for her answer, the tension in him so apparent she could nearly smell it. Her eyes glowed with amber defiance, but her pale cheeks showed her fearful capitulation. "You can confirm everything I already know about you at dinner. I'll be down in a few minutes."

Something exploded in his eyes, then died to muddied blue ashes. "Fine," he said curtly as he swiveled on his heel and went downstairs.

He was taking a last swallow of his drink when she came down, her fingers at her throat, fastening the last button of her dress. He glanced up, set his drink down on a table, then nodded at the front door. "You should bring a coat," he suggested, but there was no warmth in his tone.

Laura extracted a mohair shawl from the closet and placed it around her shoulders. "Do you want my keys?" She opened her clutch purse and felt for her key chain.

Ryder opened the door. "That won't be necessary."

"I'm not going in that truck." She pulled up short outside the door, refusing to budge off the porch.

His grasp on her arm was almost painful as he

propelled her down the steps to the drive. "My car." He pointed to the cobalt-blue Mercedes sedan parked a few yards away. Her slight gasp of surprise brought a tight smile. "It's been parked in the inn's garage. I haven't needed it before now."

"Most impressive," she said coldly. "Parisi must be quite an imposing man if you need a fancy car to clinch your association."

"Get in," he snapped, not waiting for her to get settled in the luxurious front seat as he slammed the door and strode around to the driver's side.

A stab of remorse unsettled her stomach. She was behaving terribly. She wanted to recall her remarks, but the closed look on his face precluded her offering one conciliatory word. Staring ahead of her, she bit her lip, noticeably flinching when he turned on the ignition and the car roared to life.

"For God sakes!" He slammed his hand down on the steering wheel. "We're not stepping one foot inside that restaurant until we get a few things settled."

"I thought you didn't want to discuss it." Laura was sure she would have liked to postpone what was coming.

"Exactly what bothers you most about my reports? The new dining room? The cost? Or is it the risks that scare you? That would certainly fit."

Reminding herself to stay cool, she said, "Nothing you've proposed stands a chance of working. You out-siders don't know what's involved in making changes like this. We don't need a bigger dining room, fancy furniture, and expensive wines. We cater to families on vacation who are looking for a good time."

"Outsiders." He pounced on the word, bypassing the

rest of her remarks. "That's the real issue here, isn't it? You're so close-minded you can't imagine someone who wasn't born here having a progressive idea."

"Progressive?" Laura laughed coldly. "Preposterous is more like it. All you want is to tear things down. Replace value with glitter. Lake Erie and the Cliffs will be here long after your kind moves on to greener pastures."

"You forget, Laura. I'm not going anywhere." Ryder rolled down his window and rested his arm along its edge. "Lou and I are going to bring more business to this area than it's ever seen. You locals take everything for granted and don't see that as close as the next town up the road, they're offering much more for the money. Maybe I did hope you'd realize that when we went to Kelly's Island, that you'd see the sense behind restoring quality. You asked for it by being so bogged down in the past. You won't look beyond your nose. Lou and I are working for the future."

"You and Lou." Laura nodded her head. "Two men who adore change. I'll bet he doesn't belong here, either. Why can't the two of you go somewhere else and leave this place alone?"

"Leave you alone, you mean." Ryder locked eyes with her. "I had the guts to get beyond that traditional outlook of yours and make you see things as they really are, but you couldn't stand it, could you? You want to turn down my proposals before you've heard my explanations just because they're mine."

"You've had weeks to tell me what they are," Laura said. "Did you seek out my opinion? Did you once ask for my support? No, all you did was take. Well, now you have everything, Ryder. My house, the inn, Sophie, and Will." Nearly choking, she forced herself to say it. "And you've had me, but you don't have my forty-nine percent, and you're never going to get it."

Ryder's face was gray, his eyes bleak. He didn't say anything for a few minutes, and Laura desperately wanted to get out of the car, run to her room, and give in to the pain that flowed through her in unrelenting waves.

Ryder's quiet voice shattered the tense silence. "When I was a boy, I had nothing. I learned how to survive like that and didn't even question why until my parents kicked me out of their house the day I turned eighteen. In the army, I soaked up an education like a sponge, and when I left the service, I was determined to get everything I wanted. Running my own business, I made a lot of money. It bought me a fancy penthouse in New York, this car, these clothes, and I didn't realize I still had nothing until I came here. I wanted to belong somewhere, Laura, and Merrill gave me that chance.

"Maybe you're right." He caught her eyes. "I saw you, and I wanted you so bad I would have done anything to get you. You were everything I dreamed about when I was growing up. When you looked at me with those golden eyes and I saw I could have you, I didn't even think about it. I grabbed for the brass ring before it moved out of reach. From your point of view, that was wrong. So be it. I won't take you again, but that still leaves the business. I won't give that up, Laura, not if it takes every cent I've got to make it work."

"Ryder . . . I . . ." Laura couldn't find the words, but he didn't allow her to say anything.

"Oh, I'll take things from you, Laura. Everything I can until I either own your forty-nine percent or you agree to what I'm doing with the Cliffs."

His fluid manner of speech had once provided her with a weapon to use against him. When she heard it, she'd known he was either fighting back his frustration or overwhelmed by desire, but this time neither one of those was the case. He was stating the facts, ruthlessly intent on doing whatever necessary to hold on to the Cliffs. As frightened as that made her, her resolutions were just as fixed. It would be a fight to the bitter end, for she couldn't give up her home, the inn, or her memories any more than he could.

The picture she had of him as a child did alarming things to her emotions, but she couldn't afford to be swayed by pity. There was nothing to pity in him now, and she wouldn't let him take more from her than she had to give even though she loved him. She recalled how jealous she'd been of him when it appeared he'd stolen Sophie's and Will's affections from her. Now she was glad that the elderly couple had accepted him, treated him like one of the family. He'd never had a home, not a real home, with loving people who cared about him. Perhaps the ability to give love had been one of the things he'd been forced to give up in order to survive. There was no future for the two of them together; she knew that for sure. He'd wanted her because she represented something he'd never had, but he didn't love her for herself.

"I'll never agree to something I can't believe in, Ryder." Her voice was as quiet as his.

Ryder drew in his breath and let it out very slowly. "So we both know where we stand."

"Yes, I'm afraid so." Laura agreed, turning her face away to hide the tears shimmering in her eyes.

Ryder shifted the car into gear and backed out of the drive. She realized how little she'd meant to him when he began making idle conversation, luckily not requiring any response, as they turned onto the highway and headed toward town.

After a few miles, Ryder looked across at her. "I don't suppose you'd consent to be friendly enemies?"

"For tonight?" she inquired, wondering if she was going to have the strength to sit through dinner without breaking down.

"For as long as it's necessary." The idea obviously didn't seem as ludicrous to him as it did to her. Knowing now what his plans were, knowing he'd use any weapon to get what he wanted, she immediately thought he was making the suggestion to benefit himself. She didn't dare give him anything, but couldn't think of an alternate plan.

"For tonight," she said curtly, letting him know that she was not going to declare open battle in front of the Parisis but was anticipating their private war.

"Wouldn't like to seal that with a kiss, would you?" Ryder's mouth was curved in a grin she might have thought mischievous if she didn't know otherwise.

Not wanting him to know how much the question disarmed her, she opened her purse and drew out her compact. "I think a stiff drink would be far more appropriate, don't you?" Feigning casualness, she gave her lips an unnecessary touch up of pink gloss.

"Then we're going to the right place." Ryder reached down and lifted her seat belt from between the bucket seats. "Buckle up, Laura. I have a tendency to drive too fast on deserted roads."

It was almost as if he cared about her, but she knew better. Sometimes his gallantry caught her completely off guard. She knew he was ruthless, but often he behaved like a member of the southern gentry from an earlier century, a polite gentleman not unlike those she'd read about in historical novels. It was a fascinating combination that excited her, frightened her, but always kept her attention. Perhaps initially she'd been so unwilling to consider making changes at the inn because deep down she'd sensed that what was at stake was her own preservation. He'd never respect a woman who couldn't face his challenge, and if nothing else, before they were finished with each other, she'd have his respect.

"Wouldn't it have been shrewder to forget about my seat belt, drive fast enough to crash, and hope I didn't survive?" she asked sardonically.

"Might jeopardize my own health." Ryder shook his dark head, smiled, then turned the full force of his blue eyes on her. "I can't promise to fight fair, Laura, and I will win, but you don't have to worry about your personal safety. I've learned there are better ways to get to you."

His warning came with the confident smile of a predator with its vulnerable prey in sight. She faced him bravely, not giving an inch. "Make sure I don't get to you, too, Ryder. I've learned a few things myself and won't hesitate to use them."

11

Ryder's told us so much about you, Laura." Lou Parisi, a short, stocky man in his early thirties stood up when Laura and Ryder approached the table. "I've really been looking forward to this meeting." The smile that spread across his pleasant face was echoed by the sparkle in his dark eyes. Laura didn't get the impression that he'd already formed a negative opinion of her as he gestured to the petite brunette seated at his side, then introduced her. "My wife, Maria."

Laura extended her hand across the linen-draped table to clasp that of the sloe-eyed woman, who immediately repeated her husband's sentiments. The Parisis' open smiles and friendly demeanor were far too sincere to resist, and Laura found herself returning them with equal amiability. Her hostility would be reserved for Ryder, but she still intended on getting the couple to answer a few questions.

"I understand you run the château now, Lou." Laura glanced over her shoulder at Ryder, who was assisting her into her seat. Catching the warning glint in his eye, she deliberately pressed further. "Whatever happened to Émile and Marguerite Duvall?" She was certain the question conveyed nothing more than idle curiosity, and she was undaunted by Ryder's sharp intake of breath as he sat down much too close beside her. Refusing to be intimidated by his proximity, she returned her attention to Lou, smiling politely as she anticipated his answer.

"Uncle Émile and Aunt Marguerite decided to retire, and I was the only one qualified or interested in running the château."

"You're a relative?" Laura couldn't suppress her astonishment and knew by the look on Ryder's face that he was amused by her reaction. Damn the man; he'd deliberately withheld that pertinent piece of information. Recalling their angry discussion in the car—her opinions of outsiders versus those of the locals—she knew how Ryder must be gloating. Lou Parisi belonged to a family that had lived on the peninsula longer than hers! Longing to wipe the smug grin off Ryder's face, she remembered her promise to behave herself until they were alone, but her hands curled into fists.

"My mother was Émile's sister," Lou went on, unaware of the visual byplay going on between Laura and Ryder. "My brothers and I used to spend the better part of each summer helping out at the island vineyards, but I guess the wine-making gene runs strongest in me. I went on to the University of California at Davis and earned a degree in enology."

Seeing the puzzled look on Laura's face, he elaborated good-naturedly, "Enology's just a fancy term for wine making. In the old days, the methods were handed down from generation to generation, and a lot of trust was placed in just plain luck. Nowadays, we try to eliminate the element of chance with modern technology to ensure a more consistent quality."

"It sort of shoots down the image of the little old wine maker in a dark, musty cellar, doesn't it?" Maria Parisi added, giving her husband a smile. "The first time Lou showed me through a wine cellar, I was shocked. He even made me wear a white coat like he does. The place was immaculate, almost sterile."

"That's especially true for the white wines, the kind we make at the château. You see, white wines are held in glass-lined steel or stainless-steel tanks so they're not endangered by oxidation from outside exposure. That way, they can retain the maximum beauty of their cool bouquet. The Catawbas have a—"

"Lou, you're not teaching a class back at Davis," Maria scolded playfully, then turned to Laura. "If someone doesn't stop him right now, he'll bore us for the next hour lecturing on temperatures, vine varieties, and all the other scientific technicalities. You'd know more than you ever cared to know about wines once he gets started, especially the return to excellence in Ohio whites. That's his forte."

Laura was feeling more and more relaxed in the couple's company, warming to their obvious good humor and admiring the teasing rapport they enjoyed together. Despite her earlier reservations, she liked both of them, just as Ryder had predicted she would.

Coming to Lou's defense, she said, "I know very little about wine making, but it sounds fascinating." Grinning at Maria, she admitted with a shrug, "I'm a little disenchanted, maybe. Aren't those big, picturesque wooden kegs used anymore?"

"Oh, sure, but not for the whites." Lou eagerly pounced on her question. "The reds need to breathe. In their case, oxidation is important. You see—" He stopped when the maître d' arrived at their table and presented a bottle of wine. "Has to be perfect; it's my own label," Lou said, gratified.

Nonetheless, the sparkling Catawba was offered for tasting. Lou waved aside the ritual, so it fell to Ryder. "You'd better find it acceptable," Lou threatened humorously, "or our deal is off."

Ryder took his responsibility seriously, holding out his glass as the maître d' poured a small portion of wine into it. Dramatically, Ryder sniffed at it, then held it up to the light and finally took a sip. Before swallowing, he swished it over his tongue, almost seeming to chew it before he finally allowed it to trickle down his throat. Looking very serious, he turned to Lou. "It'll do."

"It'll do?" Lou sat up straight in his chair. "You'd better say more than that, or I'll have to find an associate who can appreciate a good wine when he tastes it." Turning to Laura, he said, "Why did a classy woman like you agree to do business with a guy like him?"

Delighted to join forces with Lou in a jab at Ryder, Laura answered facetiously. "He coerced me with his charm, but I'm getting better at seeing through it all the time." It came as no surprise that Ryder took Lou's remarks in the teasing manner they were intended, while hers inspired a cold flicker of ice in his blue eyes.

The crystalline wine was poured, and Lou lifted his stemmed glass in a toast. "Here's to the successful union of the château and the Cliffs. May our wines grace every table and enhance the mellow atmosphere of that grand old house."

Not sure she liked what Lou's toast implied, Laura didn't want to ruin the convivial atmosphere but was still a bit slow in joining the others as they raised their glasses.

"Laura?" Ryder prodded, and she smiled, but their eyes met over their crystal goblets, and he knew exactly what she was thinking. When they'd finished toasting, Ryder was grinning, a noticeable twinkle in his clear-eyed gaze.

Evidently, Lou had observed their exchange. "Why do I have the distinct feeling you haven't apprised your partner of our arrangement, Ryder?"

When Ryder didn't immediately answer, Laura was more than happy to oblige. "Because he hasn't." Inclining her head in Ryder's direction, she said smoothly, "Our partnership is slightly unusual. We enjoy surprising one another. Don't we, Ryder?"

It appeared as if he were savoring a last sip of wine, but his eyes were on her as he replaced his glass on the table, his look assessing. "It makes our arrangement so much more interesting," he drawled, then deliberately turned his glance to Lou. "Actually, we didn't have time to discuss it before we arrived. Laura had a few other things on her mind that took precedence." His tone implied there was much more than business going on between them, and he cemented that impression by placing his hand over hers on the tablecloth. Both Lou and Maria noticed the intimate gesture, their understanding smiles making Laura want to shout out the truth in the most deprecating words she could think of.

She met Ryder's gaze, daring him with her eyes to

continue in the same direction and discovering that he was in a far more dangerous mood than she'd thought. She sensed he might even be ruthless enough to elaborate, and she couldn't let that happen. She pulled her eyes away from Ryder's and forced a smile as she turned to Lou. "Will someone please explain this proposed connection between our two establishments? It's not fair to keep me in suspense."

"Sure," Lou began. "You see, Maria and I want to concentrate on the wines themselves, but we also need a market and a method of showcasing what we produce. We've closed the dining room at the château, so that's where you and Ryder come in." Lou's pause was just long enough for Maria to finish the explanation.

"The amount of wine that will be ready by next year will still be small, but we should have enough to supply the inn. While the Cliffs helps us establish our reputation and gives us the market we'll need until we're able to expand, our premier wines will enhance the atmosphere of your new dining room and attract customers who are willing to pay for quality." Maria's enthusiasm was infectious, but Laura still had a multitude of questions. She had seen the figures on expansion, but there hadn't been enough explanation for her to comprehend the full extent of the plan.

She turned to Ryder for further explanation. He was leaning back, studying her closely, and Laura worded her question carefully, determined to prove to him and the Parisis that she was an open-minded person.

"Featuring local wines is a good idea, but I can't see how that will support a year-round business. We draw people in the summer, but I doubt tourists will come back in the winter for a good meal in a nice dining room. They can find that much closer to home." She looked to Maria and Lou with a plea in her eyes, hoping they'd see why she still had reservations.

"You're not the only one who had doubts." Maria's dark brown eyes expressed her understanding. "When Lou first came dancing into the house babbling about supplying wines to the Cliffs, I couldn't understand why he was so excited." Maria stopped, looking first to her husband and then to Ryder. Getting an almost imperceptible nod from each of them, she folded her hands on the table and leaned forward. "What's exciting is the concept they've developed combining elegant dining with luxurious accommodations. It took me a little while to grasp the whole idea, but now I'm as excited as they are, and Ryder has promised us reservations for the first weekend."

"Weekend? Now I'm really confused." Laura wanted more facts, but the waiter arrived to take their dinner orders, and further conversation was delayed.

Laura decided on the steak Diane, but before she could give her preference to the waiter, Ryder took her menu out of her hands. "The lady and I will have the Lake Erie pickerel." Glancing at Lou, he continued. "Make that four."

Maria didn't seem to mind having him order for her, but Laura was annoyed. It was yet another example of his highhandedness. "I'd prefer something else." Her tone was light, but the firm grasp on her thigh beneath the table was not.

"I'd like us all to sample the fish, sweetheart." Ryder's smile didn't reach his eyes. "You understand why."

"Of course." She gave in, but not before she'd dug her nails into the large hand that grasped her leg. "Always happy to oblige."

"That you are." His eyes caressed her face, lingering on her parted lips until Lou cleared his throat.

"Why don't you finish explaining things to Laura so we can enjoy our dinner when it arrives. Maria can't stand talking business during a meal."

"Perhaps Laura and Ryder don't mind mixing business with pleasure." Maria glanced pointedly at Ryder, who had draped an arm around Laura's chair. However, when she saw the angry glitter in Laura's eyes, she added hurriedly, "Unless I've misunderstood."

More than eager to straighten out the woman's misconceptions concerning her relationship with Ryder, Laura stated firmly, "Business is all we ever discuss."

The woman looked more confused than ever when Ryder grinned. "Some things don't require words."

"Ain't it the truth?" Lou's booming laughter diverted Maria's attention away from Laura's outraged face, and by the time the woman's attention returned to Laura, she had managed to regain control of herself.

"We're planning much more than a dining room." Ryder obliged Maria by continuing. "We're going to provide a weekend package that can't be found anywhere else. Our guests will be able to take a step back into the romantic past, enjoy the atmosphere of an elegant old mansion, and be treated to a sumptuous twelve-course meal, each entree accompanied by one of Lou's wines. After that, our relaxed guests can enjoy a little dancing, then retire for the night to any one of our Victorian bedrooms."

"Our Victorian bedrooms," Laura repeated dully.

"Right." Ryder nodded, and went on. "In the morning, they can choose to have a champagne breakfast in bed or a light brunch in the dining room. Are you following this so far?" He'd started his dissertation using

155

the clipped, precise accent he always used when talking business but softly drawled the last question, gazing deeply into her eyes.

Laura's brows knit, refusing to be swayed by that look. "We certainly don't offer anything like that now, but don't some of the larger chains offer similar packages?"

"Similar, yes," Ryder admitted. "But we'll have authentic atmosphere, a beautiful lake-front view, and we're small enough to concentrate solely on pleasing our guests. They'll feel like visiting royalty."

Even though they had planned to shelve the discussion during dinner, the two couples barely tasted the succulent fish that passed their lips as Ryder began describing how he envisioned the inn after restoration was completed. No matter how hard she fought against it, Laura found herself entranced by the pictures he painted of beautifully appointed sleeping rooms, a gracious dining room, and the Old World feeling of romance and charm. She had to agree that it sounded wonderful, but she still doubted its success, and more importantly, was greatly concerned over cost. Where was all that money supposed to come from? She knew it wasn't the time to bring up finances, but planned to tackle Ryder with it the instant they were alone.

After dinner, they lingered over coffee and liqueurs until the Parisis excused themselves, explaining they had a baby-sitter staying with their two young children. Before leaving, they extended an invitation to Ryder and Laura to tour the château the next day.

Ryder promptly accepted for them both. "We'd love to, Lou."

While Laura sat fuming in her chair, Lou enthused.

"Great! I'd like to show you some of the new *Vitis vinifera* I'm cultivating along with the—"

"Lou, don't start on those vines." Maria tugged at her husband's arm. "You can talk as long as you want tomorrow when we're not paying a baby-sitter." She squeezed Laura's hand. "See you around eleven. We'll have lunch and sample some more of our wines."

Seeing that Maria was looking forward to their visit, Laura, smiling, agreed to the time but lapsed into silence as soon as the other couple had walked away from the table. She and Ryder didn't exchange more than a few cursory words as they left the table, paid the check, and walked out to the car.

"You played the 'golden girl' role perfectly tonight, Laura." Ryder finally broke the silence once he had maneuvered the car out of the parking lot. "My compliments."

"For your information, I wasn't playing any role. You were right. Lou and Maria are very nice people, and I sincerely enjoyed their company."

He kept his gaze on the road that wound ahead of them, both hands relaxed on the steering wheel, but the slowly accented words he delivered warned her he was anything but relaxed. "I assume you didn't enjoy mine."

"I'd be happy to confirm that assumption," Laura intoned bitterly. "You were insufferable!"

She folded her arms belligerently across her chest and stared straight ahead. "Why do you think you have the right to make all my decisions for me?"

"What do you mean? You told Lou you liked the idea of featuring his wines at the Cliffs."

"With reservations, but that's not what I'm talking

about. I like to order my own meals and accept my own invitations. Perhaps I didn't want to go to the château tomorrow."

"Do you?"

"Yes."

"Then what's the problem?"

"I wasn't asked. That's the problem. I'm getting very tired of being pushed around, Ryder. I suggest you think twice the next time you answer for me." She was merely working up to the point where she could discuss her anger over being treated like his mistress, but before she continued, he asked another question.

"Don't you think you're being a bit petty? The fish was delicious. You said so yourself, and you want to go along tomorrow."

"I am not being petty!" Laura raged, then spied the deepening grooves in his cheeks. "Let's drop it before things get out of control."

More than a hint of a smile curved up the corners of his mobile lips. "Like they did last night?"

"Damn you!" She wasn't going to tolerate another second of his goading without retaliating. They were alone now, and she didn't have to worry about offending anyone but him. "Leave last night out of this! Believe me, there won't be a repeat. Whatever was between us is 'out of our systems,' as you so aptly put it."

"We'll see, Laura."

They'd reached the house, and Laura got out of the car as quickly as possible, nearly racing to the front door where she fumbled in her purse for her house key, hoping to get upstairs to her room without speaking to him again.

"You've always had trouble finding your keys." Her

purse was plucked from her hands and her keys extracted before she could sputter a retort. He swung the door open and followed her in, grinning as he handed the purse back to her.

She rounded on him. "See what I mean? You even appropriate my purse as if you owned it! Why didn't you just use your own key?"

He coiled his long body down until he was sitting on one of the lower steps of the stairs, effectively cutting off any escape she might have made to her room. "I forgot to bring my key, and I didn't feel like waiting around outside long enough for you to find yours. It's cold out there, and you were already shivering—or was all that shaking for some other reason?"

Laura's glare told him she couldn't be baited, but he didn't move, so she snapped, "Are you going to sit there much longer? I'd like to go up to bed."

"So would I." Slowly, his eyes ran over her from her ankles to her breasts, then upward until his indigo gaze rested on her mouth. "At the risk of sounding trite, you know you're really just as desirable when you're mad."

"Ryder, I'm not spending the night with you." She was as exasperated as she was exhausted and didn't want to stand in the foyer arguing much longer, but she sensed that he wasn't ready to end the evening. With a loud sigh, she stepped toward the wall and leaned one shoulder against it. "What do you want?"

"I want to hear what you honestly think about our association with the château."

"Haven't we discussed that enough for one night? I'm tired. I'd really like to go to bed."

"Not until I find out whether or not you're opposed to the idea or only to me."

It was clear he didn't mean to let her do anything else

159

until she had stated her opinion. "All right," she declared without enthusiasm. "I'll grant you, it sounds wonderful and could possibly be successful—somewhere else. I'm not convinced we can draw enough people to support those sort of accommodations. Nobody comes here in the winter. We'll very quickly go elegantly bankrupt."

He leaned his elbows back on the steps and looked up at the ceiling. "Laura, give me a little credit. Don't you think I researched the market? I didn't get where I am by putting establishments in the red. I do know my business."

Begrudgingly, she acknowledged that he might know his business, but she reminded him, doggedly, that she knew the area. He glowered at her, looking as if he meant to take up permanent residence on the stairs.

Completely frustrated, Laura lashed out. "These changes and renovations are going to cost a fortune! Just where is all that money coming from? I'm your partner, and I don't recall putting up one cent."

"Ah, Laura, it's too late to get into the economics behind this thing. Believe me, I've researched that, too, and can get the backing. As for your part in it, don't worry about it. I'm convinced we can work it out to our mutual satisfaction."

"How?"

"Trust me." He loosened his tie, unbuttoned the top of his shirt, and rose, each movement slow and deliberate. "If that's all, let's go to bed." He turned and started up the stairs.

New energy shot through her body, her anger erasing all signs of fatigue as she started rapidly up the stairs after Ryder. At the top, she grabbed his arm and forced him to turn around. "Trust you? Trust you! There's no way I can produce any funds for this project, and I'm certainly not going to cosign a loan. I can't believe a bank would be stupid enough to lend you money on such a harebrained scheme."

He towered over her, his eyes fixed on hers. "The money's my problem, Laura. I'm not asking you to risk anything."

"Just everything I know," she charged vehemently. "Everything I love."

Overwhelmed by her own feelings, she didn't consider that she'd stepped much too close to the fire. "Maybe you should try knowing something else," he suggested softly, grasping her by both arms and roughly hauling her against him. "Loving something else." He wrapped one arm around her and forced up her chin with his free hand. Ruthlessly, he commanded her lips apart with his tongue, appropriating what she refused to give willingly until she lost her ability to think, to breathe. She collapsed against him as he backed them to the wall, letting her feel the strength of his arousal. He broke off the kiss, moving his hand to her throat. His fingers locked on her delicate jaw as his blue eyes burned their brand on her features. "I know you still want me."

"You . . . you're crazy," Laura stammered, his touch sending all-too-familiar sensations through her body, making her want him despite her anger.

His dark lashes hid his eyes, but she could feel the intent in his body, unable to stop him as he kissed her again. "I am crazy," he murmured at her lips, his tone sounding sad. "Good night, Laura. Your weapons are much more effective than mine."

He dropped his hands to his sides and stepped away, but she was held in place by the electric-blue memory of his eyes. "One of us will break," he intoned raggedly. "God help us both if it's me."

Without looking back, he walked to his room, firmly shutting the door behind him.

12

~~~~~~~~~~~~~~~~

Laura turned the collar of her jacket up around her chin and shoved her hands into the pockets. A biting wind accompanied the mists that rolled in off the lake, but enveloped by thoughts that pulled her in opposing directions, she didn't notice the cold. The rough planks underneath her were like familiar old friends as she sat with her knees pulled up, leaning against one of the posts along the edge of the dock. How many times during her childhood had she sat in that same spot waiting for the sun to rise over the lake and burn off the morning fog? It was a peaceful time, unmarred by the sounds of boat motors or any human activity, the best time to ponder problems, draw strength from the timeless beauty of the lake, and bring jumbled thoughts into some sort of order, but that day, the insistent lapping of the heavy waves on the shore did nothing to ease her state of mind.

Adjusting her back more comfortably against the post, she glanced over her shoulder at the dismal gray vapors shrouding the corniced roof of the silent old mansion behind her. She judged that she'd been outside for hours and still hadn't managed to sort out her thoughts. Topping her list of problems was Ryder Bantel, the man, his ideas, and the seductive power he had had over her. What was she going to do? How could she go on living in the same house with him without giving in? How could she move out and give up all of her dreams? The frustrations she'd felt teaching in an inner-city school were nothing compared to that. She was being ripped apart inside and could find no solution.

A sharp breeze lifted the golden tendrils away from her face, and she closed her eyes against the mist that settled around her, reopening them immediately to dispel the images of Ryder that swiftly crossed her mind. She wanted to analyze her feelings rationally, not be swayed by enticing pictures that constantly tortured her. Make a list, Laura. That had been Gram's advice. List the pros and cons and then weigh them before making any decisions. Well, she'd listed all Ryder's pros, and there were many. He was good-looking, intelligent, successful, and had the disturbing power to turn her into jelly every time he looked at her, touched her, or spoke to her.

Now the cons. That was it! He was a con artist. Otherwise, how had he managed to gain the trust of her grandfather, the Morrisons, and the Parisis so easily? Even Tom Anderson respected his ideas and thought she should agree with his plans. I'm the only one who questions his motives, she thought dejectedly. Everyone else believes in him. Thinking over the accusations he'd thrown at her, she was beginning to wonder if she was the one who was in the wrong. Maybe she really was the obstinate, narrow-minded bigot he'd labeled her.

The vibrating boards beneath her warned her that someone else was on the pier, and she turned her head, seeing Ryder striding toward her, a thunderous look on his face and a woolen blanket draped over one arm. "You planning on sulking out here alone all day?" His angry tone forced her to her feet. As soon as he reached her, he roughly draped the blanket around her shoulders. "You could have left a note or something. I've been looking all over for you. Have you any idea how long you've been out here?"

By the tousled look of his dark hair and the shadowed stubble on his cheeks, Laura surmised, correctly, that he'd done nothing else that morning but look for her. "You're not my keeper," she reminded him, and began shrugging out of the blanket, but he tugged her to her feet and started moving her back off the pier.

"Well, maybe you need one," he grumbled, and propelled her toward the stairs, across the lawn, and into the house. Inside the warm kitchen, he firmly pushed her down on a chair. "Stay there," he ordered, then turned to the counter, poured her a cup of freshly brewed coffee, and thrust it into her hands.

The warm mug felt good in her cold fingers, but she didn't want to admit that she had stayed outside too long. She straightened her shoulders and let the blanket slip away before taking a sip of the coffee. "I was perfectly all right, Ryder. You didn't have to come looking for me. Did you think you'd upset me so badly last night I'd do something crazy? I may be a lot of things, but I'm not unbalanced!"

"I didn't say you were." Ryder frowned, sitting down across from her at the table. "I just didn't know where you were. At first, I thought you'd gone for a walk, but when you didn't come back, I went looking for you, thinking you might have had an accident. I finally found you hiding down there on the pier."

"I wasn't hiding." She finished her coffee and stood up. "If I may have your permission, I'm going upstairs to get dressed." She looked down at her faded jeans and old sweatshirt. "If you recall, you accepted an invitation for us to visit the Parisis today, and I'm hardly dressed for it." She turned on her heel and started for the hallway, but Ryder's low voice came after her.

"Laura, come back here," he growled softly, dangerously. She didn't turn immediately. "Please," he added gently. She retraced her steps but chose to remain standing. For a change, she towered over him, and the position gave her some measure of confidence. "Sit down. We don't have to be at the Parisis for hours. Or are you intending never to be in the same room with me?"

"That's ridiculous. We're still sharing this house, so until one of us moves out, avoiding each other would be impossible, don't you think?"

"Is that what you're planning to do?"

"What?" She searched his face, perplexed by his odd expression.

"Are you moving out?"

"Absolutely not," she said firmly. "To the victor goes the spoils, Ryder. I'll be right by your side when you start packing your bags."

"That's my lioness," Ryder said half under his breath, and she didn't understand his reaction at all. Sensing her confusion, he laughed. "The last time things got too much for you, you quit your job and came here. I thought you might be running away from your problems again."

She looked at a spot on the wall behind him, not willing to meet his gaze, fearing he'd see her reaction to the endearment he'd used that made it so difficult for her to address the issue he'd raised. "You wouldn't understand, Ryder. But that situation and this one are nothing alike. When it's a matter of survival, I'll do whatever's necessary."

He could take that in whatever way he chose. Still unsettled in her mind, she wasn't prepared for a serious discussion with him and sensed he was going to delve deeper. Before he spoke, she blurted, "I have some other things I wanted to do before we go to the château. I'll see you later."

"What things?"

"Am I supposed to get your approval?"

"No." As she'd hoped, the curt question sidetracked him. "I was just curious."

"If you must know," she began reluctantly, "I've decided to take a small tour of the area to find out if what you say is true. I really haven't been around here much in recent years, and things may have changed. You said you'd researched the possibilities and concluded that we should be offering more. I'd like to do a little research of my own and reach my own conclusions." Knowing he'd find something to say to that, she sat down, schooling her features so he couldn't tell what she was thinking. The last thing she expected him to do was reach across the table and take hold of her hand. Her eyes flew to his face.

He was smiling, actually smiling at her, with a genuine look of approval. "Good for you. That's the first step in making sound business decisions."

Puzzled, her brows knit. Ryder squeezed her hand. "First you gather all the data. Then, when you're satisfied with your research, you analyze it and make your conclusion." She was captivated by the vivid sparkle in his eyes. "I'll make a businesswoman out of you yet," he announced proudly, as if taking full credit for her actions. Running a hand across his jaw, he grinned. "I must look like a bear. Why don't you fix us some breakfast and I'll go shave, shower, and change. I'll join you on your tour; then we can go on to the château."

Still smiling, he abruptly rose from his chair and left the room, not even considering she might not want his company. "Fix your own breakfast!" she shouted at the door.

"Whatever." His amused baritone was swiftly receding up the stairs. "But I'm staking first claim on the bathroom."

"The man's incredible!" Laura shook both fists at the ceiling. Her movements were abrupt as she stormed around the kitchen, slamming doors. She tasted nothing of the toast and cold cereal she made for herself, cursing Ryder for having the uncanny ability to twist her into knots. One minute, she was victim of his anger; the next, she was yearning to throw her arms around him and ease his pain. He made her laugh, but just as easily he could incite her temper to the point where she wanted to scream. His tender caresses aroused her like no other man's, but he frightened her more than anyone else had ever done. As he'd promised the previous night, something had to give, and that terrified her most of all.

Although she'd told him she wouldn't deliberately try to avoid him, she did just that as she heard him leave the bathroom for his room, scampering quickly up the stairs and into her bedroom before he went down for breakfast.

They drove along a twenty-mile stretch of shore line before heading toward Heriton, a town farther up the road. Ryder said little during the trip, allowing Laura to see things for herself. She saw that most of the motels and small resorts were pitifully shabby in outward appearance and offered nothing but shelter from the elements. There was a new resort complex at the edge of town, and the contrast between it and the older, family-run businesses around Mainport was obvious, damning proof that Ryder's pronouncement about change was correct. Mainport and the peninsula were smart to make some improvements, or they would definitely have lost the greater bulk of tourist trade.

The new complex in Heriton offered both elegant and informal dining, luxurious rooms, tennis, golf, and a variety of other activities. The number of cars in the large parking lot was evidence that the establishment was enjoying a brisk business despite the fact that it was past Labor Day. Ryder told her that the complex encouraged conventions and had built the facilities to attract not only tourists but business people. Live music and dancing were provided year round in one of the rooms, basically providing a night club for the area and thereby catering to an evening crowd as well as over-night guests.

Ryder swung through the main street of Mainport on their way to the château, and again she saw the contrast between her home town and the town they'd just visited. She'd never really studied the buildings or the street before and was appalled at the run-down appearance of the majority of business establishments. There was a hodgepodge of design, decayed buildings, cracked and heaving sidewalks. It was a poor showing when compared with the neighboring town, with its charming shops surrounding a spectacular new yacht basin. Whereas downtown Heriton had an attractive new face, displaying scattered green spaces tastefully planted with shrubs and trees, Mainport looked almost the same as it had thirty years before. What might have been acceptable then was currently drab and tawdry. There were none of the inviting, quaint establishments along Mainport's bleak streets as there had been along the tree-lined drives in Heriton.

She recalled, with a painful twinge of guilt, the chamber of commerce meeting she'd accompanied her grandfather to a few summers ago when she'd been home. Heriton had already started making its changes, and there was a faction in attendance that suggested that Mainport do the same. That group, with the exception of her grandfather and a few others, had been composed of "newcomers." They had been voted down by the stronger faction of "old families," who maintained that the tourists would continue to come to Mainport and its surrounding area without the expenditure of funds to upgrade the area. After all, what did the accommodations matter as long as they were located within yards of Lake Erie and the beaches?

Laura suddenly remembered that her own grandfather had been disgusted with the attitude of so many of his neighbors. She recalled his gruff, deep voice. "They just want to take the people for whatever they can get. The Cliffs won't be any part of that convoluted thinking." Weren't those the very words he had spoken? Why had she forgotten that? Her grandfather had always been willing to listen to the other side, and his hiring of Ryder was proof that he saw the need for change. If Gramps had been willing to change, why couldn't she?

Ryder was right; she had been close-minded and was behaving like a snob. She shuddered, knowing both of her grandparents would have been appalled by her attitude. They hadn't raised her to think that a Davis was any better than anyone else, that her ideas were somehow more plausible.

She was pulled out of her reflection when Ryder opened the car door and offered his hand to help her out. He gave her an appreciative grin as she unwound her long legs from the car. The A-line skirt she'd chosen to wear slipped to midthigh before she was able to extricate herself from the seat.

"You do have beautiful legs, Laura," he drawled and tucked her arm beneath his, holding her tightly against him as they approached the handsome limestone wine cellar.

She thoroughly enjoyed the tour Lou gave them through the fermenting and riddling rooms of the historic building, where the bottles of sparkling wine were carefully hand turned at regular intervals. They viewed the underground cask room where the reds were slowly aged, and Laura listened with growing interest to Lou's explanation of the difference between Ohio and California wines, learning that American wine makers identified their best wines by grape variety. Lou was determined to make the best wine in the country and enthusiastically showed Laura his plans for expansion and modernization of the château.

By the time Maria called them to lunch at the adjoining family house, Laura was almost as excited as Ryder and the Parisis by the prospect of increasing the quantity of really fine local vintages. It gave her a great deal of pleasure to think the Cliffs could properly showcase and serve premier Ohio wine. With an enthusiasm based on knowledge and the strength of an open mind, without hesitation she joined the others in a toast to their association.

Laura offered an additional toast herself. "May our tables be worthy of your noble wines." She beamed as she raised her glass to the Parisis. Ryder kept his eyes focused on hers, and after the first sip of wine, tipped his glass slightly toward her, telling her without words that she had gone up a notch in his estimation.

After lunch, Lou took them on a tour of the surrounding vineyards, showing them the different strains of vines he'd planted among the aging, mature vines. He explained that the native *Vitis Labrusca* thrived on the mainland and they would have to take a boat over to an island to see the Old World *Vitis vinifera* that were successfully growing in the longest grape-growing season in the northeastern United States.

"Why do the more delicate vines grow better on those islands? I should think the severe winters would ruin them," Laura commented as they walked back to the château.

"It's a sort of viticultural curiosity, Laura," Lou expanded, gearing up for further explanation of his favorite topic. "You see, the water surrounding the islands keeps the late autumn warmer for about six more weeks than on the mainland. At the other end of winter, the island doesn't warm up as quickly, so the buds are delayed in opening until all danger of spring frosts have passed."

Walking between the two men, her arm unconsciously linked with Ryder's, Laura nodded her understanding. "Thanks for the tour, Lou." She extended her free hand toward the shorter man, smiling at Maria, who'd joined them when they emerged from the vineyards. "I think I've just had a minicourse in viticulture."

"Oh, no." Maria rolled her eyes heavenward. "You'll never come back for another visit."

"Yes, I will," Laura assured her, laughing. "I learned a lot I didn't know."

"Lou does know his business, doesn't he?" Maria grinned conspiratorially. "But next time we'll do something that will show a completely different side of the 'little old winemaker.'"

As soon as they'd made the short trip back to the Cliffs and passed through the familiar old pillared entrance, Laura turned toward Ryder. "Could we walk through the inn before we go in the house? I'd like to hear more about your plans."

"Sure," he agreed. "Now I think you're ready to hear them."

There was no sarcasm in Ryder's tone, and Laura didn't bristle as she might have just the day before. She'd been forced to admit, at least to herself, that she hadn't been open to change. She'd been clinging to the past for security, maybe because so much of the present had dramatically changed in such a short space of time. It was the only legitimate excuse she could think of to explain her narrow-mindedness—an excuse that was more palatable than the one she feared might be true. She had been fighting the man, stubbornly refusing to accept his ideas because she might then have to accept him. That was an issue yet to be resolved, and she knew she wouldn't be able to put it off much longer.

Standing beside the car, Ryder fished in his pocket for the mansion keys. "Here, go on over. I want to get some things that we'll need as we go through the rooms."

Laura crossed the limestone path and let herself into the deserted old house. She had a few moments to walk around the first floor before Ryder joined her, and with astonishment she saw for the first time that the furnishings in the lounge area were totally mismatched. She was so lost in her thoughts, imagining how the rooms must have looked before the house was turned into a place of business, that she was unaware Ryder had joined her until he touched her shoulder. "Ready for another grand tour?"

"Lead on," she remarked, puzzled by the long rolls of paper he had tucked under his arm and the thick folder in his hand. It was a folder she hadn't seen before. By the telltale corners of fabric swatches that peeped through the sheets of paper, she knew it held more than the facts and figures she'd previously seen. "What do you have there?" she asked.

"All in good time," he asserted. "All in good time. I'll just park this stuff in the office, and we'll look at it after we go through the rooms." They walked together to the small business office that had been created by cutting into a corner of what had once been a wide center hall. Laura silently observed the worn linoleum that covered the floor, the atmosphere that stressed utility rather than beauty.

Ryder tapped on the wall at the far end of the front lounge. "Hear that? There's a fireplace behind all this plaster, and Merrill told me there's more of them all over the first floor as well as some on the second floor. They can be uncovered and put back in working order."

"Gramps must have saved just about everything. I think there's a pile of thick boards in one of the outbuildings that are probably all the old mantels and framework. Maybe they can be used."

"That would be perfect if they're not warped or something." Ryder grinned at her and started jotting notes down on a small notebook he extracted from his back pocket. "I think you're getting into the spirit of things."

"Oh, Ryder, I really have been stubborn about all this. I think I see what you mean about the place. I've accused you of wanting to change everything, and you've only wanted to return it to its former beauty."

"That's quite a confession coming from you. I've got an apology to you, too. I was so caught up in my ideas for the place that when you showed up, all I could think about was you'd prevent it all from happening. I didn't realize I wasn't giving you a chance to understand what I had in mind. I can see now why you probably envisioned neon signs, textured plaster, and cheap furniture all over the place."

"Something like that," she agreed with a smile.

As they walked through the house, the list of repairs grew. Some of the furnishings could remain if they were repaired and refinished. Caught up in the excitement of turning the Cliffs back into the gracious showplace it had once been, Laura was ready to climb the narrow, steep stairs to the huge attic and rummage around for furnishings that might be salvaged, but Ryder stopped her at the attic door. "You'd ruin that pretty skirt you're wearing. We'll tackle the attic some other time." He took her hand and led her back down to the office where he spread out the conceptual drawing he'd received from the architects, showing her how he thought the rooms should eventually look.

"Now I see what you wanted to do with the wicker. I like the small solarium idea, but who's going to keep all those plants growing?" she asked as shoulder to shoulder they studied the drawings.

"You are," he commented, then squeezed her shoulder. "You wanted to be a part of this, didn't you?"

"You're from a farm. You should be the gardener. I'll find something else to do that doesn't require a green thumb." She regretted her flippant choice of words as soon as she saw the bitter twist to his lips.

"We'll work out the responsibilities later," he said, then started rolling up the blueprints.

They had been getting along so well it was difficult for Laura to acknowledge the issues that still separated them. Wanting to hang on to the companionable atmosphere they had enjoyed all afternoon, she swiftly exclaimed, "I only meant that as a joke. Don't be hurt."

His frown grew in intensity, and his laugh was harsh. "Meaning what, Laura? Don't tell me you think comments about my background still bother me. That poor boy from Georgia grew up long ago."

"Then why . . ." She was floundering, not knowing what to say that wouldn't make matters worse. "I thought you were glad I'd changed my mind, that I like your ideas for the Cliffs. Ryder, everything was fine until

I made that comment. If I didn't hurt your feelings, why aren't we still discussing the plans?"

The silence lasted so long she thought he wasn't going to answer her, but finally he walked around the desk and sat down in the swivel chair. "Tell me, Laura. How do you picture us working together? What do we do? Do we go on sharing the house, but not a bed, while we refurbish the inn? And what happens later when the inn is ready to reopen? Are you willing to let things go on as they are forever?"

"I'm willing to compromise, Ryder," Laura saw he was remembering their confrontation the night before. "I've given in on the main issue. I can't see why we can't reach some kind of agreement on a little thing like living arrangements."

"I see." Ryder locked his hands in front of him. "So, you consider the main issue between us is making changes at the inn. I'm afraid I don't look at it like that, Laura. You see, I haven't worked you out of my system as it appears you have me. Once we commit legally to this thing, I'm not going to be able to live in that house without making love to you. I told you I wouldn't be satisfied until I had everything. You were included as part of the deal. Are you telling me you didn't understand that when we outlined our intentions?"

"Part of the deal?" Laura repeated dumbly. "The inn, Ryder. We were both stating our feelings about the inn. Our personal relationship has nothing to do with that."

His eloquent glance told her that as far as he was concerned, it had everything to do with it. He stood up from the chair and walked across the room to where several cardboard boxes were lined up against the wall.

He reached inside one and removed a framed picture. Handing it to her, he waited until she'd recognized herself, then said softly, dangerously. "I want it all, Laura. One hundred percent of that golden girl and the inn. If you won't give me all of it, then one of us will have to leave."

There was nothing loving in his tone, and when her glance shot to his face, his features were ruthless. "Leave?" Laura cried. "I'll never give up the inn, and you can't—"

"Force you to sell?" Ryder broke in savagely, stalking to the door, his face a frozen mask. "You're right. I can't do that any more than I can force you to want me, so I'm leaving before I do something I'll really regret."

"Ryder!" She ran to the door, but he had already dissappeared down the hallway. Racing through the lobby, she pulled open the main doors, desperate to stop him, but he'd somehow slipped into the garage, and by the time she reached the driveway, he was speeding toward the gates. "I love you, Ryder," she screamed, but the words dissolved in the gray mists that were rolling in from the lake.

13

Laura looked down at the picture album opened in her lap, then up at her surroundings. Seventy years earlier, her great-grandmother had danced on the polished wood floors. The room had then been a ballroom but was now the vacant lounge at the inn. In her mind's eye, Laura could see the ladies twirling in white lace dresses, their voluminous skirts flowing around them as they whirled in time with the music. Her glance shifted outside to the wide veranda, and she pictured her ancestors strolling across the rolling green lawn in front of the mansion. What would they say if they could see her now, sitting alone on a green vinyl chair that she had pulled up to the window? The golden light from crystal chandeliers had been replaced by fluorescent tubes, the waxed floors covered by service-able linoleum, the lavish furnishings by utilitarian benches.

Ryder hadn't returned, and as the hours passed, she had become more and more afraid that he might not come back. She had tossed and turned all night, wondering where he was, wondering what she should say to him if and when he returned. When daylight came, she went back to the inn and sat by the windows in the deserted lounge, trying to imagine what it would be like to direct the renovations they had planned together without him. She had no desire to do anything without him, and that shocked her. Once, the Cliffs had meant the world to her, but without Ryder, the inn seemed lifeless and empty.

Telling herself she was only feeling sorry for herself, she sought to revive some of her earlier enthusiasm by taking out the old family albums, but when she looked at the pictures of her family, all she wanted to do was cry. She'd done a lot of fruitless crying during the night, but all it had accomplished was to increase the puffiness beneath her eyes.

She lifted a faded picture out of the album, staring down at the first Laura Davis, her great-grandmother. "What would you have done? Would you have let yourself become part of a business deal?" she asked, but all she heard in response was the harsh echo of her own voice bouncing off the walls of the lounge. She closed her eyes, remembering Ryder's last words. He'd said he couldn't force her to want him. Was it possible that he loved her? Is that why he had stormed out in a rage? Because he thought she would never love him in return?

"I have to do something," she whispered, then replaced the picture inside the album and closed the book. Getting up, she played a hunch and went to the phone, dialing the Parisis' number, but when she found she was right, that Ryder was with Lou and Maria, she lost her nerve. Instead of asking to speak to him, she left a curt businesslike message with a perplexed Lou, stating a time when she expected Ryder to come to the inn for an important business meeting.

Several hours later, Laura sat down behind the desk inside the office at the inn. Pressing her fingers to her throbbing temples, she took a deep breath. She had heard Ryder's car come up the drive and knew he was over at the house, probably changing clothes. In a few more minutes, she would have to face him and state the terms she knew were necessary for her own survival.

Trying to control her anxiety, she gazed around the office. Her grandfather's pictures were back up on the walls, but her belongings were scattered throughout the rest of the room. Hoping to present a picture of businesslike sophistication, she'd swept up her hair in a severe style and worn a tailored jacket over her translucent silk blouse. She smoothed down her skirt as she tried to get comfortable on the swivel chair behind the massive oak desk. Glancing at her watch for the hundredth time, she bit her lip. How much longer would he make her wait? What was he doing over there?

She jumped when she heard the lobby doors swing open with a resounding crash. It was Ryder, all right; she'd recognize that determined step anywhere. He was stalking down the hallway, making the sharp turn toward the office, almost at the door.

"This had better be good," Ryder pronounced angrily, striding into the room, his blue eyes cold as they cut into her face. "That phone call to Lou sounded oddly like an order, and I don't follow your orders, lady."

"Won't you have a chair?" Laura gestured calmly to the seat she had placed in front of the desk. "This shouldn't take very long."

His eyes narrowed on her smooth features, a muscle leaping beneath the taut skin of his jaw as he stepped back and abruptly lowered his tall frame into the chair.

"I wanted to talk with you." Laura didn't meet his eyes. "You had your say last night, and as your partner, I'm demanding equal time." She leaned back in her chair, striking a nonchalant pose that was as false as the unemotional tone of her voice.

"We won't be partners much longer," Ryder said, cold fury icing his words. "State your business, Miss Davis. I've got to catch a flight to New York in four hours, and I don't want to miss my connection out of here. If it's a legal fight you want, you'll get it. I plan to meet with my attorneys."

"I believe you and I can work this out on our own." Laura felt the tension working its way up her spine but refused to expose her real feelings until she'd gained what she wanted. "Dragging in our attorneys won't be necessary."

"I think it will, and we both know why." Ryder leaned forward in his chair, resting his elbows on the arms and locking his hands together in front of him.

"I don't think I do," Laura insisted tightly. "Why don't you explain it to me."

She didn't know whether it was her tone or the words themselves that got to him. When he addressed her again, the soft drawl was in his voice, the drawl that meant she had gone too far. "Damn you. Just what are you after? You've got nothing to offer that's worth my giving up one share of the business."

"Don't I?" she retorted provocatively, then could

have cut out her tongue. He went pale, his hands clenched together so tightly that his knuckles appeared white. Without meaning to, she had taunted him, reminding him that only the day before he'd been impressed with all she had to offer. That day, she had planned to make her move so quickly that it would all be over by then, but somehow, even having mentally prepared herself for that moment, she hadn't counted on what the sight of him in his three-piece business suit would do to her. He could still destroy her with one look, challenge her beyond reason, ignite all her senses, but suddenly she felt more defensive than ever before. There was not a hint of softness about him, and she had been foolish enough to provoke his anger.

She knew she was already in way over her head, but there was nothing left to do but get on with it. She should have come up with some other way to make her point, not attempted to maneuver a man who knew all the angles, but it was too late to back out now. "I believe I have come up with an arrangement that might be acceptable to us both. I have certain conditions, of course."

"An arrangement?" Ryder's laugh was harsh and disbelieving. "And what about my conditions? Did you forget about those overnight?"

"I want to discuss my conditions, not yours." Laura refused to deviate from course. "Compromise is essential in any relationship."

He raked his hand through his hair, leaning back in his chair and crossing his arms over his chest. He looked ready to explode but had enough control remaining to give her his attention for a while longer. "Get on with it, then. I can't wait to hear your idea of a compromise."

His eyes raked down her body, leaving her in no

doubt of his feelings, but it wasn't the time to respond to that heated look. She swallowed hard, then plunged on. "I've written down my requirements. If you accept these conditions, we can include a clause like this in our new business agreement."

"Business agreement?" Ryder rasped. "I have no intention of entering into any kind of contract with you, and I'll get out of the one I'm in if it takes every cent I've got."

"This won't cost you a dime, Ryder," she insisted shortly, then revealed her nervousness by clearing her throat. Her fingers were trembling as she lifted the paper she had prepared before he'd arrived. "I . . . I, Laura Davis, agree to sign over my forty-nine percent interest in the Cliffs, its grounds, and the involved homestead on the condition that one Wilson R. Bantel agrees to my proposal of marriage and exchanges the vows of matrimony before witnesses at a mutually agreed upon date, precluding the necessity for the aforementioned agreement."

The written words blurred as Laura endured the strained silence that followed her statement. It went on and on until Laura thought she might scream. She didn't dare lift her head, didn't dare look up and find that he didn't want her under any conditions. She heard his chair scrape, heard him stand up, and she closed her eyes tightly, clasping her hands together so she could dig her nails into her palms and let the sharp pain divert her from the agony searing her heart.

"Laura?" Ryder's voice came from beside her, but he didn't touch her, remained standing a few feet away.

She had to face him. There was no other choice. Later, she'd break down, relive the humiliation of his refusing her proposal. But that would come later, after he left. Let him leave! she cried silently. Don't make this worse. Please. The tears she'd promised herself not to shed were already poised to fall, and when she lifted her head, her eyes were brimming with liquid pain. "You . . . you don't have to say anything, Ryder," she whispered. "I . . . I just wanted you to know how I felt."

"I need you, too, Laura." He came slowly toward her, the dumfounded look on his face telling her how much she had shocked him. "I love you, but yesterday, when I told you how I felt, you couldn't talk about anything but the inn. Why do you want to marry me, Laura? I need to hear that it's not just because you're not sure you can manage this place without me."

"Oh, Ryder." Laura didn't wait to hear more, jumping up from the chair and throwing herself into his arms. "I love you so much, I'm not capable of doing anything without you. This is your home, and when you aren't here, I have nothing."

She lifted her face from his jacket, given courage by the feel of his strong arms stroking her back. Their eyes met, his still questioning and hers filled with the answers he'd longed to see. "You never told me you loved me, Ryder." She placed her fingers over his lips, lovingly tracing the firm contours as she gazed into his eyes. "Am I more than the brass ring? The golden girl you dreamed of when you were a boy? Part of a business deal?"

His fingers grasped her hand, drawing it to his chest so she could feel the unsteady rhythm of his heart. "You're everything, Laura. My lover, my friend, my harshest critic, and my strongest supporter. You're my life, Laura. I thought I'd been hurt when my folks told me to leave, but it was nothing compared to the pain I felt walking away from you last night."

"You didn't have to leave," Laura cried, tears of happiness replacing the misery that had welled up behind her eyes, cleansing tears that wet her cheeks and soothed her soul. "I called you back, but you didn't hear me."

"No, I didn't," Ryder agreed, his voice rough with emotion. "If I had stayed, you wouldn't have proposed to me just now. I would've made love to you until you agreed to every damned thing I wanted." When her expression showed that she might have enjoyed such a predicament, he shook his head and drew her to the chair. Quickly sitting down, he pulled her onto his lap. "Even when it's legal, I'll still want this." He covered her lips, as he sought to show her beyond words how much he needed her.

They drank of each other like parched victims that had been stranded in a void of perpetual anguish. As their tongues and lips exchanged countless love words, their hands searched for each other, touching what both of them had feared might not be within reach again. It was a very long time, a healing time, before they were willing to break the reassuring contact of their bodies clasped together in mutual longing. "You didn't see it," Laura murmured, smiling tenderly.

"See what?" Ryder inquired, his attention on divesting her of her jacket. When he saw that she was wearing nothing beneath her sheer blouse, he sucked in his breath. "You didn't need to propose. All you would have had to do was take your jacket off. I would've been all yours within seconds."

His fingers were doing a quick job of unfastening tiny satin buttons as she attempted to regain his attention. "Ryder"— she laughed, grabbing hold of his wrists—

"all you would have had to do was look up there." She pointed to the wall.

The expression on his face was worth all the hours of suffering she'd lived through without him. She followed his gaze to the frame, predominantly larger than all the others hanging on the paneled wall. Taken at Kelly's Island, the blown-up picture showed Ryder staring down at the glacial grooves. Feet planted apart, he had one hand on the rail, the other jammed into the pocket of his pants. His hair was ruffled in the breeze, his handsome features relaxed. His eyes were strikingly blue, enthusiastically alive. She had captured the strange half smile he had turned on her that day, a melancholy smile that had troubled her, but she'd never been given the opportunity to ask about its cause. She did so now. "Don't you like having your picture taken? I hope that's not the problem, because this family has a habit of taking lots of pictures."

His smile was heart-rending. "This family can have all the pictures it wants. You're the first person who's ever taken a picture of me, Laura. I used to stare up at all those pictures of you and wallow in self-pity. Silly, huh?"

"Not silly, human," Laura reassured him, resting her head against his shoulder. "Next time, we'll get someone to take a picture of us together." She reached up to stroke his face with tender fingers, then slipped her arms around his neck. She embraced him tightly, telling him he belonged to her and she'd never let him go again.

"I love you, Laura," he whispered softly when she finally allowed him a deep breath.

"Can I take that to mean you approve of my version of our agreement?" she asked, the flecks in her eyes a brilliant shade of gold. "We won't have to call in the lawyers?"

"I'd like to spend some time in private negotiations." Ryder slid his hands inside her blouse, beginning a tantalizing journey upward from her waist.

"How much time?" Laura demanded, trying to sound offended but failing miserably as his fingers stroked higher. "If we wait, you could lose interest in this venture."

"You'll always control my interest, love," Ryder murmured, and with that tender reassurance in mind, they began the negotiations.

YOU'LL BE SWEPT AWAY WITH SILHOUETTE DESIRE

$1.75 each

1 ☐ James
2 ☐ Monet
3 ☐ Clay
4 ☐ Carey

5 ☐ Baker
6 ☐ Mallory
7 ☐ St. Claire

8 ☐ Dee
9 ☐ Simms
10 ☐ Smith

$1.95 each

11 ☐ James
12 ☐ Palmer
13 ☐ Wallace
14 ☐ Valley
15 ☐ Vernon
16 ☐ Major
17 ☐ Simms
18 ☐ Ross
19 ☐ James
20 ☐ Allison
21 ☐ Baker
22 ☐ Durant
23 ☐ Sunshine
24 ☐ Baxter
25 ☐ James
26 ☐ Palmer
27 ☐ Conrad
28 ☐ Lovan

29 ☐ Michelle
30 ☐ Lind
31 ☐ James
32 ☐ Clay
33 ☐ Powers
34 ☐ Milan
35 ☐ Major
36 ☐ Summers
37 ☐ James
38 ☐ Douglass
39 ☐ Monet
40 ☐ Mallory
41 ☐ St. Claire
42 ☐ Stewart
43 ☐ Simms
44 ☐ West
45 ☐ Clay
46 ☐ Chance

47 ☐ Michelle
48 ☐ Powers
49 ☐ James
50 ☐ Palmer
51 ☐ Lind
52 ☐ Morgan
53 ☐ Joyce
54 ☐ Fulford
55 ☐ James
56 ☐ Douglass
57 ☐ Michelle
58 ☐ Mallory
59 ☐ Powers
60 ☐ Dennis
61 ☐ Simms
62 ☐ Monet
63 ☐ Dee
64 ☐ Milan

65 ☐ Allison
66 ☐ Langtry
67 ☐ James
68 ☐ Browning
69 ☐ Carey
70 ☐ Victor
71 ☐ Joyce
72 ☐ Hart
73 ☐ St. Clair
74 ☐ Douglass
75 ☐ McKenna
76 ☐ Michelle
77 ☐ Lowell
78 ☐ Barber
79 ☐ Simms
80 ☐ Palmer
81 ☐ Kennedy
82 ☐ Clay

YOU'LL BE SWEPT AWAY WITH SILHOUETTE DESIRE

$1.95 each

83 [ ] Chance	93 [ ] Berk	103 [ ] James	113 [ ] Cresswell
84 [ ] Powers	94 [ ] Robbins	104 [ ] Chase	114 ☐ Ross
85 [ ] James	95 [ ] Summers	105 [ ] Blair	115 ☐ James
86 [ ] Malek	96 ☐ Milan	106 [ ] Michelle	116 ☐ Joyce
87 [ ] Michelle	97 [ ] James	107 [ ] Chance	117 ☐ Powers
88 [ ] Trevor	98 [ ] Joyce	108 [ ] Gladstone	118 ☐ Milan
89 ☐ Ross	99 [ ] Major	109 [ ] Simms	119 ☐ John
90 [ ] Roszel	100 [ ] Howard	110 [ ] Palmer	120 ☐ Clay
91 [ ] Browning	101 [ ] Morgan	111 [ ] Browning	
92 [ ] Carey	102 [ ] Palmer	112 [ ] Nicole	

SILHOUETTE DESIRE, Department SD/6
1230 Avenue of the Americas
New York, NY 10020

Please send me the books I have checked above. I am enclosing $_____.
(please add 75¢ to cover postage and handling. NYS and NYC residents please
add appropriate sales tax). Send check or money order—no cash or C.O.D.'s
please. Allow six weeks for delivery.

NAME_____

ADDRESS_____

CITY_____ STATE/ZIP_____